JOURNEY TO AN 800 NUMBER

JOURNEY TO AN 800 NUMBER

by E. L. Konigsburg

ALADDIN PAPERBACKS

First Aladdin Paperbacks edition June 1999

Copyright © 1982 by E. L. Konigsburg

Aladdin Paperbacks
An imprint of Simon & Schuster
Children's Publishing Division
1230 Avenue of the Americas
New York, NY 10020

Also available in an Atheneum Books for Young Readers hardcover edition.
Printed and bound in the United States of America
10 9 8 7 6 5 4 3 2

The Library of Congress has cataloged the hardcover edition as follows:
Konigsburg, E. L.
Journey to an 800 Number
SUMMARY: Bo learns about kindness love, loyalty, appearances,
and pretense from the unusual characters he meets
when he is sent to stay briefly with his father
after his mother's second marriage.
ISBN 0-689-30901-5 (hc.)
I. Title
PZ7.K8352Jo   [Fic]   81-10829
ISBN 0-689-82679-6 (pbk.)   AACR2

For Mae and Sid,
Leonard R.
and Michael B.
sister and brothers in law
and under the skin.

JOURNEY
TO AN
800
NUMBER

1

When my mother married Mr. F. Hugo Malatesta the First, she sent me to stay with my father while she went on a honeymoon. To my mother he was always your father, the camel-keeper. My mother divorced him because of his camel.

"What kind of a life is it for a wife and child to drive around the country with a camel," she had said. "What kind of a life is it to spend your time getting people to pay to ride his hump?"

My father's camel has one hump; it is a dromedary. Bactrians have one more hump and more hair. My father's camel also has a name. Ahmed. I don't know if Ahmed means anything as a name. As a camel it means a lot to my father, the camel-keeper.

"We have lots of fresh air and sunshine," my father had said.

"Half the time we go to shopping centers and half the time those are under a roof and air-conditioned."

"Aw, Sally," Father had pleaded, "in small towns we're always in some pasture. We move around a lot."

"That's the point, Woodrow," Mother had said. "What kind of a life is it for a child to move around a lot, living in a camper, driving an animal that doesn't even look interested? I could understand a dog, Woodrow, I really could. A dog wags its tail at you. A dog comes when you call it. A dog shows interest."

"You can't ride a dog, Sally. What would I do with a dog, Sally? No one would pay money to ride a dog—not even a big one, an English sheepdog, say, or a St. Bernard."

"That's my point, Woodrow. I want a dog."

"We can't manage a dog and a camel, Sal."

"That is also my point, Woodrow. I want a dog and a house. And meals from china plates instead of from Styrofoam containers. I don't want a life that is tied to a camel."

My father said, "Ahmed has been good to us, Sally."

My mother said, "Ahmed has been no better to us than we've been to him. I've gone my last mile for that camel."

"What do you want me to do?"

My mother said, "I want to stop roaming, Woodrow. I want to settle down. Bo here is going to start school in a few years, and I mean for him to have a regular routine when he does, and I mean for him to have kindergarten before that. I do not want Bo to be a nomad."

Father thought. "Tell you what we can do, Sal.

We can park the trailer in a regular trailer park. We can even take off the wheels and put it up on blocks. Then I'll take Ahmed only as far as I can to be home on weekends. I'll be a commuter."

"You don't seem to understand. I want regularity."

"Commuting is regular, Sally."

"But the money isn't. I want a regular house and a regular income. I want to know that I'll have the same amount of money coming in next week as this. You have to decide, Woody. Either me and Bo and a regular job or your camel."

"But, Sally . . ."

"I'm not going to argue. You know that I don't like arguing with you, Woody," Mother had said.

In the United States it is difficult to get someone to take a full-sized camel off your hands, and my father had said that he didn't want to give Ahmed to a zoo. Ahmed was, he said, not a wild animal. He was, he said, *trained*. He had a name.

So Mother left. She took me with her. I was four years old at the time.

First we went to the junior college at Morrisville, New York, where Mother got an associate degree in hotel management. Mother finished her degree when I was ready to start school. She then took the job of executive housekeeper at Fortnum School in Havemyer, Pennsylvania, outside of Philadelphia.

She chose that job because it came with a cottage on the school grounds and free tuition for me when I would get to seventh grade. In the meantime I went to the neighborhood school, and since Fortnum was in a nice neighborhood, my elementary education was quite satisfactory.

Mother's job involved ordering light bulbs and bathroom supplies and keeping track of linen and food for the dorms. She didn't actually clean the rooms or cook the food; she supervised the people who did. We developed quite a nice life for ourselves, even though we never got a dog. I did not mind not having a dog. I am not your basic animal lover.

We called ourselves Sarah J. (her) and Maximilian R. (me). Some people called me Max. I always told people that the R. was just an initial and didn't stand for anything, but it wasn't, and it did.

I was born after a rainstorm at 2:00 p.m. on May 15 in Taos, New Mexico. The rainstorm is important because my father had promised my mother that he would name me according to an old Indian custom. He had promised my mother that immediately following my birth, he would walk blindfolded outside the hospital. (A friend of mother's would guide him.) Once outside, he was to take off the blindfold. The first thing he saw would become my name. The first thing my father saw was a rainbow. That was what the R stood for. My real name is Rainbow Maximilian Stubbs: the Maximilian because Mother thought it meant a lot. People began calling me Bo right away. We spelled it *Bo* instead of

Bow so that no one would confuse my name with the first syllable of *bow-wow*. Both my parents always regarded it as a good omen that the first thing that Father saw after I was born was a rainbow. So do I. After all, there was a chance that I could have been called One Dog Squatting.

After we settled in Havemyer, no one called me Bo. Except Father. He would come to Havemyer about once a year, but he would not stay at our house on the Fortnum school grounds. He stayed at a campground outside town. Ahmed stayed with him. He drove to our place in his truck.

One year he asked me if I would like him to bring Ahmed to Fortnum to give the students rides. Free. I told him I didn't think it was a very good idea. I didn't tell him why. He didn't ask.

One of Mother's duties was to set up for tea and cakes when the Board of Trustees of Fortnum met. Mother would put on one of her good dresses and pour a second cup of coffee for anyone who wanted a second. She would stay in the background looking quiet and pretty, but listening. She knew that if the Board of Trustees started talking about cutting down on expenses, she would have to change the light bulb order from hundred watt to sixty and the toilet paper from two-ply to scratchy.

Mr. F. Hugo Malatesta the First was appointed to the Board of Trustees of Fortnum School in the fall, and he noticed mother at the first meeting he attended. Mr. Malatesta's wife had died two years before. His children were all grown. Both of his sons had gone to Fortnum School. One of them was a lawyer. The other was a stockbroker. His daughter was married to a lawyer and played tennis and raised money for worthy causes that got her picture in the paper quite a lot. Mr. Malatesta was near the age of retirement and well into the age of grandchildren. He had five grandchildren. One of them, F. Hugo Malatesta III, was two years younger than I. The F. stood for Francesco, pronounced Fran-ches-ko, but never used.

F. Hugo called mother on the telephone the afternoon following the evening of that first meeting, and he asked her to marry him in the spring. Mother said that she would marry him in the summer. She said that she would be happy to. Mother explained her reasons to me: I would be starting Fortnum in the fall, and she wanted me to go as a regular day student and not as the child of a servant of the school. Mother had been around the school enough to know that the children of faculty—and Mother's rank was lower than faculty—have a name. They are called UW's, which is the abbreviation for United Way, which means charity. Mother said she didn't want me to be a UW when I entered Fortnum.

I looked forward to Mother's wedding, and I looked forward to moving into Mr. Malatesta's house and having Mother drive me to Fortnum from there. The house had six bedrooms and four bathrooms, a gardener, a housekeeper, and I think they sent their laundry out.

Mother looked forward to her wedding, and she looked forward to her honeymoon. Even though this was her second marriage, she told me that it was her first honeymoon. Mr. Malatesta was taking her on a cruise, and that was why I was to stay with my father, the camel-keeper.

I was to meet him in Smilax, Texas.

I asked Mother to get my school blazer before she left for her honeymoon cruise. She reminded me that at my age I could easily outgrow a jacket in a period of a month. I told her that I didn't think that I would. She got me the jacket.

She and Mr. Malatesta drove me to the airport. Before I boarded the plane, Mr. Malatesta gave me fifty dollars, five tens. He didn't make any big fuss giving it to me. He just said, "Spend it foolishly," and I told him that I would.

I got off the plane in Smilax wearing my navy blue school blazer with the Fortnum School crest on the breast pocket. It was the first Saturday in August, and when they wheeled the steps up to the plane and opened the door, I thought that someone—God—had made a mistake. There was no out-of-doors there. There was no air there. I felt that I was breathing mayonnaise. I was sweating down to my insteps and up to my eyelids. The heat made everything look wavy, but I still was able to spot my father from the top of the airplane stairs.

He was standing behind a chain link fence with a lot of other people waiting for the plane to arrive. I had not seen him in one month more than a year, but he was easy to pick out of a crowd. He wore the same red bandanna around his neck and the same black hat that looked like Pinocchio's that he had worn on his last visit to Havemyer. My father is what adventure books call swarthy, and he adds a big black mustache to that. He is a hairy man. He has black hairs that grow like boogers out of his nose and his ears if he doesn't cut them with a scissors.

Father spotted me and waved. I walked down the stairs and across the tarmac very slowly. I could not walk fast. The air seemed more solid than the asphalt I walked on. Actually, the asphalt was soft; I could feel my shoes sticking to it the way they do when you're walking down the aisle in a really crummy movie. I could feel the navy blue wool of my blazer sop up sweat like a paper towel that was winning a contest in a television commercial.

I reached my father and extended my arm for a handshake, but Father reached over and—hot as it was—hugged me. "Hi, Bo," he said, "it's good to see you. Very good."

"I'm called Maximilian now," I answered.

"Well, Max, did you have a good flight?"

"The food was like a TV dinner."

"So you've already had lunch?"

"That's what they called it."

Father studied me awhile longer, reached his arm around my shoulder and said, "Let's go collect your luggage."

The terminal was air-conditioned. Blasts of cold air were pushed through vents in the ceiling. The wind chill factor in the terminal building was minus fifteen degrees and felt good. As we waited for the luggage to come off the plane, I stood directly under one of the vents and allowed my sopping blue blazer to blow in the wind. Soon the conveyor belt began moving, and soon after that pieces of luggage came riding around on it.

"If you'll point out what belongs to you," Father said, "I'll lift it off."

I didn't point it out, I lifted my two suitcases off the belt by myself and picked one up in each arm and said, "Shall we go?"

Father reached down to take one suitcase from me, but I held on. I started walking, holding one suitcase in each hand. Before I reached the door, I thought my hands would break off at the wrists, but I carried both pieces to the door without his help.

Father held the door open for me, and I walked through, my suitcases banging my knees, my shins, my thighs. Once outside, the hot air wrapped around me again. Once again I began perspiring like a lower species of animal. Sweat locked into the weave of my blazer and vaporized. I knew that there was a cloud of steam lifting from where I stood. And it was only one-thirty in Smilax.

"You wait here," Father said. "I'll get the truck and pull around."

I waited there on the sidewalk watching the sun flick off the windshields of the cars as they pulled up to pick up their passengers. I thought that I would (a) go blind, (b) rot like a piece of fruit, (c) faint. Father arrived before I did any of the above. He asked me if I would like to take off my jacket, and I told him no, not at all. He shrugged and drove us to his trailer camp out on Highway Six.

He gave me some cold Coke and asked me if I would like to see Ahmed. I told him no thanks and asked him where I was to put my things because I had some letters I wanted to write.

"I do my writing at the kitchen table," he said. "And you'll sleep in the bottom bunk unless you prefer the top."

"The bottom will do quite nicely," I said.

Father said that he had to go to Pickwick Mall because he had advertized that Ahmed would be there between three and six. He invited me to go along, but I told him no thanks, that I thought I had mentioned that I had some correspondence to take care of, and he said that yes, I had mentioned it, but he thought that maybe I would like to go with him and postpone writing my letters, and I told him that postponing things was not something I was in the habit of. He told me to help myself to anything in the refrigerator or the pantry and that he would be back about seven-thirty. He mentioned our going out for our first supper.

The minute he walked out the door, I took off my blazer. I turned the air-conditioner to COLDEST and turned the vents so that they blew right over me as I threw myself across the lower bunk and fell asleep.

I woke up because I sensed a strange light coming into the trailer. It was only the afternoon slant of the southern summer sun. It didn't look like ordinary light. It looked as though if you touched it, it would punch back. I felt trapped by the blaze of light falling in slats through the windows of the camper.

I walked outside. My father's camper was a runt among the others in the park. A one-room aluminum job with a slope on the back. It looked more like a giant turtle than a trailer. There were almost no people outside. I walked around and saw through the windows the pale blue flickering light that told me that television was on. I couldn't hear anything, for all the trailers had air-conditioners thundering away at one window or another.

I went back inside my father's trailer feeling the chill blast of his air-conditioner. I started to shiver and decided that I should probably get something to eat. The refrigerator was a little half job with a tiny yellowish light like a single bulb on a Christmas tree. I found some bread and some beer.

The bread was stale; I didn't know if the beer was, for it was the first I had ever tasted. I sat at the kitchen table tearing off pieces of bread between my teeth and swigging beer and wondering how many afternoons I would have to spend this way. I knew that I would not be going to shopping centers helping Father sell camel rides.

I opened my suitcase and took out my paper and my ballpoint pen. I intended to write my mother a beautiful letter full of descriptive phrases and no split infinitives. I intended to write her every day, so that at the end of the month she would have a chapter of letters that would tell her what I thought of the meaning of life. I would give her permission to publish them when she asked.

I felt chilled again. I poured the rest of the beer down the drain and thought some hot tea would taste good, but it seemed like a lot of work to make it. I turned the air-conditioner to OFF and still could not warm up. I climbed under the covers of the lower bunk and fell asleep on and off, half-waking only long enough to notice that the brazen light had softened and moved to the other side of the trailer, and then to notice that the trailer was dark. Finally, I was awakened by a sound. Father had returned. I sat up.

"Hi," Father said. "Did you get your letters written?"

"My letters?"

"Your correspondence."

"My correspondence. Oh."

"That's all right. You were probably tired from your trip. I've got Ahmed fed and settled. Now, how about us, Max? Ready for dinner?"

I said all right.

So I got my blazer, and we went. Father drove around Smilax, and we didn't speak very much. Smilax is mostly highways with quick-food chains, gas stations and motels and no houses more than one-story high. And the evening air, although not cool, at least moved. Or we moved, and it seemed to. Father pulled up at a cafeteria named Sweetbriar's. We went through the line, and the things did look good. I took three more items than I could eat. I didn't seem to have much appetite once I smelled the food up close. Father asked, "Don't you like it, Max?"

"It's all right," I said. "Mr. Malatesta took Mother and me to a restaurant on the top of the First Guaranty Bank Building in Philadelphia. If you walked around to look through each of the windows, you got a view of the whole city below. They had candles on every table and white tablecloths and napkins. Cloth, not paper. And the waiters wore tuxedos." Father said nothing, but he looked interested, so I continued. "It's a private club, and you have to wait on a waiting list and have people recommend you before you're allowed to join. And even then you have to pay money, a thousand to join and some every month. That's *besides* paying for the food."

"How was the food?" Father asked.

"Excellent," I answered. "Why?"

"Oh," Father said, "I heard that most times those restaurants on top of tall buildings have what you might call *food with a view* instead of food that tastes good."

"Just because you've never been and likely never will be is no reason to put them down."

"Nobody ought to put them down," Father said, "because then they wouldn't have anything at all to recommend them."

"Very funny," I said.

"If you don't want your Jello, mind if I take it?" Father asked.

I pushed it over toward him. He dipped his spoon in it and held it up where it wiggled in front of his eyes, then he ate it. He played that way with every spoonful. I didn't say anything, and neither did he.

We didn't speak all the way back to the trailer park either. Father had opened the windows of the truck again, but I closed the one on my side. I felt cold. And my stomach was being unkind; it was rolling around like a maniac salami, pitching back and forth, even when the truck was stopped for a red light.

The first time I threw up was against the front

wheel of the truck just after Father arrived at the trailer park.

Father led me toward the kitchen sink in case I was going to make a second deposit. He supported me and held my head. "You have a fever," he said.

"A fever?" I yelled. I put my hand on my forehead and said, "I'm burning up. I've caught some dread disease. I must have a hundred and six. Where's your thermometer?"

"No one gets a hundred and six fever. I don't have a thermometer," he said.

"You don't have a thermometer?" I asked. "How can you appreciate how sick I am? How will you know when to call a doctor?"

"I think you have the flu."

"Isn't that dread?" I asked.

He touched my forehead with his lips. "I'd say you have about a hundred, a hundred and one," he said.

"Your mustache is probably insulating your lips from feeling the full heat," I said.

Father handed me two white pills. "Here, take these aspirins with a big glass of water and go lie down."

The lying down part sounded good. I did as he suggested. I remember Father reaching to the upper bunk and taking down a cover and covering me and putting his hand to my forehead again. Next I remember waking now and then to the sounds of music. I thought at the time that it was the TV; later when I was fully awake, I saw my father sitting in the kitchen area strumming a guitar. A grown man amusing himself with a guitar. He needed a shave. His mustache was ragged, and even from a distance I could see the hairs poking out of his nose.

He saw me awaken. "Well, hello there," he said.

"Did you get the thermometer?" I asked.

"Well, no," he said. "Except to feed Ahmed, I haven't left the trailer for two days."

"Ahmed," I said, throwing myself back down on the bed. "Ahmed!" I repeated, putting as much disgust in my voice as I could manage. Then I realized what he had said. "Two days?" I asked.

He smiled and nodded and strummed his guitar.

"Do you mind telling me what I've been doing for the past two days?"

He continued strumming and said, "You threw up a lot."

I waited for him to continue, but he didn't. "What else?"

"Not much. You slept. You moaned in your sleep. You peed in a bottle." He strummed his guitar the whole time he said this making it like a folk song.

"Did you call a doctor?"

"No doctor did I call." Strum, Strum.

"Do you realize that I have lost two days of my life?"

"Me, too." Strum, Strum.

"Can't you tell me about them?"

"You took liquids and you slept and you peed in a bottle." Strum, Strum.

"Lost," I said. "Two whole days of my life lost," I said to the ceiling.

"Time flies when you're having fun," Father sang. Then he laid down his guitar and came over to my bunk. He sat on the edge and laid his hand on my forehead and then ran his hand slowly down my face. Then he rested the back of his hand under my chin. "Welcome back, Bo," he said.

"Name's Max," I said. "Maximilian."

It was not until the middle of the week that I had any appetite or energy. I woke up one morning and instead of finding Father rattling around or reading or strumming his guitar, I found a note Scotch-taped to the refrigerator door. Half door. The note said: *Ahmed and I are at summer school fair. Back about four.*

That suited me just fine. Now I would have time to put my thoughts in order. The five days since I had arrived had had no nights, no days, just long sleeps interrupted by crazy dreams (really crazy). I decided that first I would walk around the trailer park and get some fresh air and exercise.

I left the trailer door unlocked because I didn't know where Father kept the key and besides there was nothing in the trailer worth taking—except, perhaps, Father's guitar, which wasn't even a Martin or a Guild. I decided to solve that problem by taking the guitar with me as I got my fresh air and exercise.

The minute that I opened the door, the hot air hit me like someone had dropped a hood over my head. But I was determined. If men could fight for the Alamo in Texas, I certainly could walk around a trailer park carrying a guitar that wasn't even a Martin or a Guild.

It was not easy, but I managed to walk in one direction for fifteen minutes and then start back. Except that I got lost. To an untrained eye every third trailer looks alike, and when I thought that I was going to collapse, I finally knocked on a door to ask directions. No one answered. I had to go to four trailers before I found one lady-of-the-house at home. She had a small baby and was actually nursing the baby when she answered the door. I had never seen anything like that in my life, and I must say that it didn't give me a very high opinion of the trailer park class of people. To nurse a baby as if it were the most natural thing in the world.

I guess the woman was asking me for the second or maybe the third time, "What do you want?"

I asked her if she could please direct me to the trailer of Woodrow Stubbs.

She thought a minute and then said, "Haven't heard of him."

I hated to say it, but I knew that I must. "The camel-driver," I said.

"Oh. Ahmed's daddy," she said.

"No, mine."

"Well, yes." She smiled.

"He lives in the transient section."

"Transient?"

"The people who keep their wheels and hook up by the week." She then gave me directions, and I thanked her and left, and her kid never disattached itself the whole time.

Her directions were pretty good because I followed them and got back. I noticed that the transient section where my father lived was not as nice as the non-transient. The trailers were smaller and there were no pretty flower or vegetable gardens around them. It wasn't until I got back and hung up Father's guitar and was lying on the bed that I realized that I had no idea where Ahmed stayed. I didn't care. I was exhausted, and I fell asleep until Father woke me.

"Hey, Max," he was saying, "how about let's go out for a while? We'll stop for a bit to eat. The fresh air will do you good."

"I don't think there is a pint of fresh air in all of Smilax," I said.

"Yeah, it's pretty humid. I was scheduled to start working my way north, but we got held up."

"*We* got held up. *I* got held up. I got sick."

"Yes, it's been too bad. I had to cancel two bookings, and today I could only make one instead of two. I had to drive Ahmed."

"Don't you always drive Ahmed to where you're going?"

"He hadn't had any exercise for days, so I drove him to the kindergarten."

"You mean you *rode* Ahmed?"

Father nodded.

"You mean you rode a camel through the streets of town?"

"I guess people have been riding camels longer than they've been riding cars. Longer than horses, even."

"You must look pretty silly," I said.

"Maybe I do. But besides giving Ahmed his exercise, it's good advertising." Father stood up. "I know a good place for us to eat tonight. We'll celebrate our last night in Smilax at Mom's Ranch Kitchen. They have something close to home-cooking. How about it, Max? Do you think we can push off tomorrow? I figure we'll stop in Dallas tomorrow night."

I told him that I was ready. I had seen all I want to see of Smilax, Texas, for the rest of my life.

2

It was still dark when I heard Father get up. I watched him wash and shave and waited to see if he would cut the hairs out of his nose and ears. He did. He sat at the edge of my bed after he was finished, and he shook me. He spoke very softly, "I'm going to drive over to Ahmed's now. I have to get him into the truck before I hook on the camper. Do you want to get dressed and see him or do you want to sleep some more?"

"Sleep," I said.

It wasn't easy to sleep. There were the sounds of Father driving off, then returning, and the sounds of the camper being hitched to the truck. Finally, there was a tug at the camper and the sounds of Ahmed gurgling and bawling like a retarded cow. The whole process must not have taken too much time because before it was even light, we were well out on the highway. I could feel the uninterrupted roll of the wheels. I decided to get up.

I looked out the front window of the camper and there I saw Ahmed's behind, his tail swinging before my eyes. The rear end of a camel is a sight only a camel of the opposite sex, only a camel of the opposite sex in heat, could find exciting. A camel has got to be the ugliest beast ever assembled. Even dinosaurs, which didn't work out at all, had a certain dignity. They may have been bulky, and they may have been dumb, but they weren't dumb *looking*. Ahmed's behind was—among other things—bald.

I got dressed and sat looking out the back window where the view was all interstate instead of inter-hind-legs.

We stopped in the parking lot of a gas station/ restaurant. I got out of the camper and Father got out of the truck cab. We met at the truck bed alongside Ahmed. Father was patting Ahmed and whispering words of comfort that sounded like "good boy" and "ni-i-i-ce fella."

"He's bald as a kumquat," I said.

"It's summer. Camels shed in the summer. Two summers ago I was at this town in north Florida and there was a young woman who was a weaver. She came way out to the west end of town to see me when she found out that I was there."

"How did she find out?" I asked. "Did she live downwind of his litter box?"

"I was written up in the paper."

"Really?"

"Sure," Father said. "On a slow news day, they put me in the local news."

"On the comic page?" I asked.

"Usually on the first page of the second section. That's where the local news is. Sometimes in the feature section."

"What do you do with them? The articles, I mean."

"I read them, of course."

"What do you do with them after you read them?"

"I wrap the garbage in them. Just as I do with all the other newspapers. Can't save too much when you live in a camper. Well, anyway, back in Florida two summers ago there was this woman weaver and she came out to see me to ask me if she could brush down Ahmed and collect his hair. She was making some kind of weaving. She had a black poodle and she was saving his hair, too, and she wanted to make a pattern in tan and black. She came every day and gathered up Ahmed's hair, and since the summer had begun, he was shedding and she got bushels of hair. I never did see her work, but I venture to say it was more tan than black."

"What did she make with it?"

"It was to be a wall hanging, she said."

"That's a relief."

"Why?"

"I thought she was weaving something to wear."

"When you consider how much a camel's hair sweater costs, or you realize that the second best artists' brushes are made of camel's hair, you would know that camel's hair is nothing to sneeze at."

"Unless you're allergic," I said.

"Very good," Father said. "You are a clever boy." He looked over at me and grabbed my shoulder in that sort of hug of approval that he had.

We were at a cafeteria again. This one was sectioned off so that one side was for professional truck drivers. We went to the civilian side. After filling our trays, I picked out a booth that was across the aisle from a mother and daughter. The daughter looked fifth-graderish. I knew they were mother and daughter because they looked like the petite and queen-sized versions of the same product, except that the mother was dressed in a pants suit and had her hair pulled back with a scarf and the daughter was dressed in jeans with her hair hanging loose all around and falling over the table.

After we sat down, I jabbed my thumb in their direction and said to Father, "You could probably weave that into a room-sized rug unless she eats it with her eggs."

The girl was holding a fork in midair and reading the paper while her mother was eating with the best possible manners. "Sabrina," the mother said, "you better finish up if we're going to make Dallas before evening."

Without looking up, Sabrina said, "Would you hand me the scissors, please?"

The mother reached into her pocketbook and took out a small pair of scissors, "Find something for your collection, dear?" she asked.

"A two-faced cat," the girl answered. She cut

something out of the paper and handed the scissors back to her mother. "It's got a picture. Two faces. One head. It eats with both mouths." She held up the clipping.

"Very nice, dear," the mother said.

"I still can't find out anything about Renee," the girl said.

"Well, dear, sometimes no news is good news."

"I'll have to check again in Dallas. Sometimes these small towns put only the national news and the local gossip in their papers." The girl then looked over toward us and said, "Excuse me."

I was so busy pretending that I wasn't listening that I kept digging right into my hash browns.

Father said, "Yes?"

The girl said to him, "Have you heard any news about Renee, the girl who had her hand cut off by a New York subway and the doctors sewed it back on?"

"Can't say that I have," Father answered. "Maybe my son has."

I had rested my fork somewhere in midair, and my mouth was open—not for food but for astonishment. I hoped that everyone thought *food*.

Father said, "Max, have you read anything lately about Renee, the girl who had her hand cut off by a New York subway and the doctors sewed it back on?"

I said, "I have not only not heard anything lately, I haven't heard anything *firstly*."

"Renee is a very talented flute player from New

York City who went to a special high school for talented children . . ."

The mother nodded and said, "The High School for Music and Art."

"You have to be very talented just to be allowed to go to school there. It's free if you live in New York."

The mother nodded and said, "They have dancers and musicians and artists. Of course they're *all* artists, but I mean, painters. They are all very talented. They come from all over the city."

"That's why they have to ride the subway. And Renee was just a few weeks away from graduating when someone pushed her off the subway platform and the train ran over her hand and cut it off, and a subway guard put the hand in a plastic bag and rushed it to the hospital right along with Renee, and the doctors sewed her hand back on."

"An eleven-hour operation," the mother said, nodding again.

"No one knows if she can ever play the flute again. But you should always remember to put any part that's cut off—even if it's just a finger—into a plastic bag and take it to the hospital with you."

"Took the doctors hours and hours just to clean the flesh around where the hand was cut off," the mother said.

"If you can pack the cut-off part in ice after you put it in the plastic bag, that's best."

"Have they found the guy who shoved her?" I asked.

"Man or woman," Sabrina said, "they haven't found who did it. I was hoping you'd have some news."

"Sorry we can't help you out," Father said.

I looked over at Father, and I realized that he really was sorry. He would have liked to have had some news of Renee to tell to this Sabrina and her mother.

Sabrina's mother said to her, "C'mon now, dear, you'd better eat up if we're going to get to Dallas." She looked over at Father and said, "We're going to a convention in Dallas."

"So am I," Father said.

That was the first I heard about it. "What convention are we going to?" I asked.

"Travel agents," he answered.

"Why?" I asked.

"The Mideast Airlines have a big booth at the Convention Center, and they've hired Ahmed to be in the booth to attract people. Sort of a visual aid."

"You mean they've actually invited Ahmed indoors?" I asked.

"It's a convention center," Father explained. "That's like wide open spaces except that there's a roof over it. You'll be glad to know it's air-conditioned." Father turned to Sabrina and her mother and explained, "Ahmed is my camel."

The mother said to Sabrina, who was back to reading her paper, "Sabrina, dear, this gentleman, Mr. . . ."

"Stubbs," Father said. "Woodrow Stubbs and my son, Maximilian."

"Sabrina, Mr. Stubbs and his son have a camel. Now, isn't that interesting? We've never met camel owners before."

"Owner," I said.

"What's that, dear?" the mother asked. "It's Maximilian, isn't it?"

I nodded.

"I'm Lilly," she said, "and this is my daughter, Sabrina."

Sabrina nodded, took another bite of toast, wiped her mouth and got up. She was not very tall, and she was as skinny as a ball point pen and as straight. Very fifth-graderish. She hitched up her jeans because she didn't have any figure to help hold them up, and she pulled down on her jersey, and she wasn't flattening anything underneath the jersey when she did. She was what you might call "going-on-pretty." Except for her eyes, which were hazel and as wide as the CBS eye, and they were already pretty. Maybe beautiful. And her nose and her mouth fit under her eyes just right, not too big, and not too small, just right. And they were pretty. So were her teeth and her smile, when she did. Her hair was brown and nothing to brag about. "Is your camel here?" she asked.

"In the parking lot," Father answered.

"We'll look for him on our way out," Lilly answered. Then Lilly tugged at the top of her pants suit the way that Sabrina had tugged at her jersey. Lilly's movemens were like an instant replay of Sabrina's—exactly alike but a little slower. The two of them looked like Lilly and Lilliputian.

I don't look anything at all like my father. He is, as I said, swarthy with black curly hair; his eyes are the color of tobacco stains. I have straight light brown hair and blue eyes. My father is hairy; I am not; my father is heavy-boned; I am not. And I think I am going to be tall; my father is average.

"When you're in Dallas, why don't you stop by the Mideast Airlines booth and say hello to us," Father said.

Sabrina said, "In case you hear anything about Renee, we'll be staying at the Fairmont." She smoothed the clipping about the two-faced cat over her pants leg and followed her mother to the cashier's desk.

Father turned and watched until they were all the way out the door.

When we got back to the truck, I found a note on my side of the cab. It said, "I like your camel. Sincerely, Sabrina." I folded it up and put it in my hip pocket. I said to my father, "I didn't know you were hired by an airline."

"Ahmed was."

"How much are they paying you?"

"Two-fifty a day. From nine to nine."

"Two-fifty? You make more with two kiddy rides."

"That's two hundred and fifty," Father said.

"That's profitable," I said. "Have you ever been in Dallas before?" I asked.

"Sure."

"Does it have one of those restaurants on top of a tall building?"

"Probably does."

"Is the Fairmont a tall building?"

"Pretty tall."

"Do you suppose it has a restaurant?"

"Might have. We'll plug into our trailer park and clean ourselves up and go on over."

"Do you have a jacket and a necktie?" I asked.

"Somewhere I think I do."

"And I don't think they require a hat," I said.

We had to tether and feed Ahmed before we went to the campground community showers to get a real good soaking shower. Father took time to trim the hairs in his nose and ears. We got to the Fairmont right around seven-thirty, which I thought was late for supper, but which seemed to be rush hour there. They had a restaurant, with linen napkins and candles on the lobby floor. The head waiter asked us if we had a reservation, and we said no, and he said that he was terribly sorry but that he couldn't let us in. He mentioned that there was a convention of travel agents headquartered there, and they were booked solid. He told us to try the coffee shop on the opposite side of the lobby.

As we passed the hotel registration desk, I was wondering if I should mention to Father that maybe we ought to stop by to say hello to Sabrina and Lilly, but I didn't say anything because the thought came to me that I didn't know their last name, and I couldn't tell anyone at the desk who it was I wanted to say hello to. I looked over at Father and thought that maybe it would be better if we went to some McDonald's or some other place where a camel-keeper, even without a Pinocchio hat, looked more at home.

As we approached the elevators, I saw one open, and who should get out but Sabrina? She looked as if she didn't know whether or not to say hello. I thought that she didn't recognize me in my blue blazer with the Fortnum School crest on the breast pocket. She looked different, too. Her hair was curled and she had on a long dress and on her—you should excuse the expression—breast was a tag that said: HELLO. I'm Sabrina Pacsek. The Sabrina Pacsek was handwritten; the rest was printed.

"Well, hi there," I said.

She looked at me and said, "Oh, hello."

"Remember me," I said. "The restaurant this morning." I pointed to Father. "He has the camel you like."

"Oh, yes," Sabrina said. "What are you doing

here? I thought I saw the camel's truck hitched to a house trailer."

"You did," I answered.

"We came here to eat. Father and I are connoisseurs of fine food. We enjoy eating at the better establishments whenever we arrive in a city that has one."

"So you're both gourmets," she said, studying Father. I could tell that she knew that he wasn't.

"We like good food," Father said.

Sabrina said, "I hope you'll excuse me. Mother is expecting me. There was a mix-up with our convention registration. Mother is at the convention desk straightening it out now."

Father said, "We'll go with you. I'd like to say hello to Lilly."

Sabrina started to protest, but Father put a hand between her shoulder blades and steered her around. Around the corner was Lilly, bending over a row of tables that had a long felt cover over them. Lilly was talking to a man who sat behind a stack of folders, and a woman who sat behind a stack of envelopes. She was saying, "That's perfectly all right, Mr. Hogarth. Mistakes do happen."

The woman behind the stack of envelopes had a pair of eyeglasses on a chain. She put them on, looked through their bottoms and examined the HELLO badge she handed Lilly. "How do you pronounce your name?" She asked.

"Pah-check," Lilly answered, pinning the badge

just north of her bosom. "It's Czechoslovakian."

"Well, Mrs. Pacsek, I'm glad you had that letter."

"So am I. Sabrina, my daughter, is . . . Oh! here she is now."

Sabrina had edged her way over to her mother's side. "Mother," she said, "look who I ran into in the elevator."

Lilly turned toward us, smiled and said, "How delightful!" She said to the woman with the glasses on a chain, "Please excuse us. Some old friends have arrived."

"How nice that your daughter will have someone her own age to keep her company."

"Why, yes," Lilly said, turning around and fitting herself between Father and me. She reached an arm across each of our backs. "Let's go in to the opening reception and toast our reunion."

And before we could do much about it, she had one of her hands between each pair of shoulder blades and was pushing Father and me toward a large room that opened off the lobby. She let the pressure off my back as soon as we got inside the entrance to the room. She said to Sabrina, "It'll be an open bar, dear. You can fetch you and Maximilian a Coke. Mr. Stubbs and I will meet you back by this door about five minutes before the banquet."

The light in the room was not too good, but even before Sabrina returned with our Cokes, I noticed that we were the only two non-adults in the room. And I noticed something else that I mentioned to Sabrina. "Why does everyone except you and your mother have his name badge printed instead of written by hand?"

"That was the mix-up over the registration," she said. "They had forgotten to put badges in our Conference Kits, so we had to write ours by hand."

We sat down at one of the small tables that they had set up along the back edge of the room. "Heard anything more about Renee?" I asked .

"No. There wasn't anything in the Dallas paper about her. But there was one thing worth clipping."

"What was that?"

"About this five-year-old girl who died an old woman."

"How can a five-year-old die an old woman?"

"A disease called Cockayne Syndrome made her age at the rate of fifteen years for every year she lived."

"I don't believe it."

"You better. I have the clipping in our room. C-O-C-K-A-Y-N-E Syndrome. There's no known cure. Actually she died of the chicken pox for which there is also no known cure. But people don't usually die of chicken pox. It's just that when you have Cockayne's Syndrome you can't fight off a simple childhood disease like the chicken pox because although she was only a child, she was about . . ." She started counting her fingers. ". . . about . . ."

"Seventy-five years old."

"You good at math?" she asked.

"Not bad," I answered.

"Where did you get the camel?"

"I didn't get it. It's my father's."

"Where did he get it?"

I shrugged. "I don't know."

"How can you not know?"

"I think he had it before I was born."

"Haven't you ever asked?"

"No, I haven't."

"Why?"

"My mother and father are divorced."

"Aren't everybody's?"

"But I live with my mother. This is the first time—ever—that I've stayed with my father. Except, of course, for the time before they divorced, and I hadn't even started school then."

"Where do you live usually?"

"Havemyer, Pennsylvania. It's near Philadelphia. I'm going to go to Fortnum School in the fall. That's a private school. College prep."

"I've been to a convention in Philadelphia."

"Did you go to the restaurant on the First Guaranty Bank Building? It's a private club."

"No. Mother and I actually avoid those restaurants. The view is good, but not the food. Food-with-a-view. Besides, we had all the banquets and luncheons of municipal employees to attend."

"Municipal employees? I thought your mother

is a travel agent. This is a convention of travel agents."

"My father was a municipal employee."

"I thought your mother and father are divorced."

"*Now* they are," she said. "Hungry?" she asked.

I admitted that I was.

She led the way across the room to where there was a long table set up with hors d'oeuvres and bowls of pretzels and nuts. We helped ourselves generously. I saw Father and Lilly talking to a small group of people. Father still did not look as if he belonged. Most of the men wore colored sports jackets. There appeared to be a lot of pink plaid. The women ran to rhinestone eyeglasses and bright blue chiffon, and three-fourths of them looked as if they had gone to the same beauty parlor. There were enough nests of curls on top of enough heads to make a bird sanctuary. Lilly, too, had one. She hadn't had one at the restaurant.

"Did your mother go to the beauty parlor?" I asked.

Sabrina glanced up at Lilly and popped a cracker into her mouth and licked her forefinger and her thumb as daintily as if it were good manners. "It's one of her wigs."

"One of them?"

"Yep. She carries a supply. When we arrive at a convention, she reads the kind of people they are and puts on a fitting head." She looked over the crowd.

"She was right. Lilly always is. That is her once-a-week-and-spray-it-in-place hairdo. Very common among convention wives. Lilly likes to blend in with the crowd."

I wondered if my father could. I wondered if my father even realized that he didn't.

Sabrina asked me if I'd had enough to eat, and I told her that I had. "The hors d'oeuvres are usually better than the banquet," she said.

"You sound like you go to a lot of conventions."

"It's a way of life," she answered.

We were back at the row of tables against the wall. We found an empty one. Empty except that there were six glasses on it and a puddle under each. Sabrina stacked them together and carried them to another empty table, took a napkin and wiped up the sweat rings and dumped that napkin on top of the stack of glasses. "Sit," she invited. I did. "I'm going to go to exhibit hall tomorrow just to see your camel."

"My father's camel."

"What's its name?"

"Ahmed."

"I would appreciate your finding out how your father got him."

"Are you going to write my father up in your collection of freaks?" I asked.

I thought she would immediately say no, but she didn't. She thought a minute and said, "I don't think so. It will depend on the facts."

"What facts?"

"The facts of the case, of course."

"Could you please explain what you mean by that?"

"A freak is a freak despite what he does. An eccentric may do outlandish things, but he has a choice. I don't collect eccentrics. They interest me, but I don't collect them."

"Maybe someone has been doing something eccentric for so long that he can't help himself doing it. Maybe it's no longer a question of choice. Maybe it's a question of compulsion. Like maybe someone has a compulsion to collect freaks and can't help herself anymore."

"Not the same thing."

Father and Lilly were coming toward us, and Sabrina said, "I'll see you tomorrow." She left me there with a hundred things more I wanted to say but with time for only a polite good-night. Father said good-night, too.

"Did you have a nice visit with Sabrina?" Father asked.

"She's better company than Ahmed." Father raised his eyebrows but did not look hurt.

"Did you have a nice visit with Lilly?"

"That woman sure knows how to laugh," Father said. "She must have pronounced her name a hundred times. Nobody knew how to pronounce it. She just made a joke of having to repeat it."

"You would think that if she's a travel agent, at

least one other travel agent would have known her," I said.

"Maybe she's new to the business," Father said.

"Maybe she is."

"Are you very hungry?" Father asked.

"Not very."

"Me neither. What say we just pop into Sonesta's and have a bowl of chili?"

"I'd prefer something even less than that," I said. The travel agents had taken the edge off my appetite, and it had not cost us a cent.

The next morning Father and I got up at five a.m. and put on boots and rain slickers and went to a car wash halfway between Dallas and Fort Worth. It was one of those do-it-yourself places where they supply power hoses and vacuums. Before we could take Ahmed to the Convention Center, we had to hose him down.

We pulled the truck into one stall, and we jumped out of the cab and put the planks down so that Ahmed could be led into another stall. Camels spit when they're mad. Ahmed spit. We tethered him to a post. Camels kick when they're mad. Ahmed kicked. I don't think there is any animal alive, including the rhinoceros, that has less class than a camel.

Father said, "Don't vacuum him. There'll be too much hair clogging up the machine and it will burn the motor out."

We hosed Ahmed down, and as much as you can tell from the look of a camel, I guess he liked it. He always looked sleepy. Father was cooing to Ahmed, ready to lead him out of the stall, when a carload of kids pulled into a booth two down from ours. The first one to notice Ahmed told the others, and they came over to our booth six abreast.

"Hey, Pop," one said to Father, "how many miles to a gallon?"

You could tell that Father had been asked the question before. He said, "Can get speeds up to ten miles an hour for only a gallon of feed. Under ideal conditions."

"No pit stops or shit stops, eh?" the kid said, walking toward us.

Another one of them started toward Ahmed; that one reached out his hand and said, "Is your nose ticklish?"

Father said, "I wouldn't try that if I were you." The boy kept on coming, and Ahmed spit. It landed with a plop on top of his sneaker. It was a king-sized hawker that dripped down the toe of his shoe. The kid looked down and said, "You better clean that off, old man. Nobody's camel is allowed to spit on me."

Father reached into his pocket for his hanky, and I pushed him back. "I'll clean it off, Father," I said. And I did. I turned the hose on, and sprayed the spit from the fellow's shoe. It also wet his pants legs. It also wet his shirt, and the shoes, the pants and the shirts of four of the others. "Th-e-e-e-re you go," I said. "All gone."

The first kid started toward me, and the five others were not far behind. I backed up toward the stall. Father untethered Ahmed, and instead of leading him toward our truck, he led him toward the center of the pack of boys. A camel is a loose, uneven assembly of parts; you never know which part will fuss or for how long. When a camel spits or when a camel kicks, it is a good idea to watch out. There is no telling whether something wet or something heavy will land. Ahmed began kicking. He kicked with all four legs in about twelve directions. It was impossible to escape from one side of him or the other. You could have found an area of quiet about a yard or so from his head, but he could spit that far. Or you could go to his rear, where I won't mention what indelicate thing he could do. All in all, Ahmed cleared a pretty good bit of living space for himself. Those six guys went back to their car about as mad at Ahmed as Ahmed was mad at them. But the dumb beast had won. I wanted to stand outside and say something sarcastic that they would remember the rest of their lives, but Father pushed both me and Ahmed back into the booth. He locked his arms around me so that I couldn't move. Before I could ask, I knew why. The guys revved up their car and came zooming in for us, and had we not been protected by the posts of the booth, they would have rammed us senseless or run right over us.

We waited until we saw their car disappear down the highway before we emerged.

"I would like to wash the truck, too," Father said.

"Let's get out of here," I suggested strongly.

"All right," Father said in an unhurried way, and in an unhurried way he loaded Ahmed back into the bed of the truck.

I was shivering with rage. I took off my slicker and my boots and put on my blue blazer, which I had neatly folded on the seat of the cab. I began to feel a little more like myself.

Father said, "There's always one wise guy in a bunch of kids like that."

"One out of every six?" I asked.

"I don't know the exact percentages, but it seems to me there's always one."

"Maybe they just don't like camels."

"I guess you could understand that," he said.

"Tell me, where did you get Ahmed?"

"Your mother and I were living in New Mexico, around Taos. I had a big old ranch house outside of town where people came and stayed awhile and then left. Some stayed for years. Couples. Odds and ends of people. We farmed. We made candles and sandals and sold them to tourists in the town of Taos. Anyway, one of the young men who came and stayed had a camel. The boy's name was Lucky Blue, and the camel was Ahmed. After Lucky Blue had been with us about six months, he left. He left in the middle of the night with a young woman but not Ahmed. Lucky Blue and Dove. The girl he took away with him was Dove. Of course, those were probably not their real names. No one used a real name back then."

"When was this?"

"Back in 'sixty-eight, 'sixty-nine."

"Well, I never did learn where Lucky Blue went or where he had gotten Ahmed. But I couldn't neglect Ahmed or abandon him after Lucky Blue left."

"Was I born yet when Lucky Blue arrived?"

"No. But you were when he left."

"Were you and Mother hippies?"

"How do you know about hippies?"

"Havemyer, Pennsylvania, is not the end of the world, Father. I can read. I know about hippies and flower children back in the sixties."

"To answer your question, I guess I would have to say that yes, you were a flower child and your mother was a hippie. A college drop-out, nice middle-class family. Have you ever met your mother's folks?"

"No. Mother told me they died in an automobile wreck the year you two got divorced."

"Oh."

"What about you. Were you a hippie?"

"I don't think so. I am considerably older than your mother. Twelve years older. I had been living in that big ranch house outside Taos for a long time before kids started coming in and crashing at my place. The house was mine. We sold it to buy the camper. I gave the rest of the money to your mother when we got divorced. I figured she'd need some money to go to junior college and get started in a more ordinary life." He stared at the road as he drove. "I gess I'm not *really* a hippie. I guess you'd have to call me an eccentric."

"And I don't collect eccentrics," I mumbled.

"What was that?"

"Just repeating something I heard last night."

When we arrived at the Convention Center, we were directed to the loading entrance. Once there, our truck got in line and waited for some official to go over our papers to let us in. Father showed the man the contract he had from the Mideast Airlines. The man checked it over and gave us each a badge with a blue ribbon that said EXHIBITOR. He told us that would be our pass for getting on and off the floor.

"Don't you ever get to go in the front door any place?" I asked.

"The camper," he answered.

"Only has one door," I said.

"Yes, it does," Father answered.

When we arrived at the loading platform, Father let down the gate of the truck and hoisted himself up to place the ramp from the back of the truck to the loading platform. Ahmed had emptied his bowels all over the back of the truck.

"I'm glad to see that," Father said.

"Do you think there's a market for it in Dallas?" I asked.

"No," Father answered. "It means that Ahmed won't do it on the way to our booth. I'll let you stay with Ahmed, and I'll come back and clean it up."

"Do you expect Ahmed to do it right on the exhibition floor?"

"Of course. Ahmed always does it."

"What are you going to do about it?"

"What I always do about it. I sweep it up with a broom and a shovel, and I put it over there." He pointed to the covered wooden box in a corner of the truck bed.

"What's in there?"

"Just sand right now."

"Soon to be flavored with . . ."

"Let's go. We're holding up the others."

With Ahmed spitting and gurgling, we joined the parade of strange creatures moving toward the exhibition hall.

There was a man who was almost seven feet tall dressed in a turban and pantaloons and carrying a sword that adventure books call a scimitar. He headed toward the Air India Booth. There was a bearded midget dressed in short green pants; yes, a leprechaun. He went to the Irish Tourist Bureau. Three men in black tights lined up under a paper dragon that said Cathay Airways and snaked around the whole exhibition floor. There were men dressed as chefs who worked behind ovens advertising, "A

Gourmet's Tour of Italy Only $1299, New York Departure." There were Indians: Peruvians, Mexicans, Zuni; Wagons: Conestoga, horse-drawn, stage coach; Towers: of London, the Eiffel, water; Carts: donkey and golf. Besides the three-man dragon weaving in and out, there was a young girl in pigtails and pink ribbons, an almost-bra and very short pants who skated around the floor all day. She carried a sign that said: "Venice, California, is where it's really at."

"I don't think her grammar is correct," I said to Father.

He smiled after her as she skated past. "Let's just hope they notice the sign at all," he said.

"I wonder if the Mongolians will have an idiot in their booth?" I asked. Father gave me a look that told me not to repeat that remark.

The representatives from Mideast Airlines were waiting for us at their booth. Now, there was swarthy, all right. They looked glad to see us. I guess that if you had just a plain booth, you felt pretty left out. They introduced themselves. One of them had two gold teeth right in front. He produced a harness and saddle that were gorgeous. Part of the gear was a saddlebag made like a small Oriental rug. That rigging made even Ahmed look not-too-bad. Father saddled him up, admired him at length and then left to clean up the truck. After he left, one of the men handed me a burnoose and an Arabian headdress. "Please to put on," he said. "We have also one for daddy. More authentic."

"What's the matter? Haven't you ever seen a blue-eyed Arab before?"

"Is jacket," he said, pointing to the Fortnum crest over my breast pocket. "Is very British, no?"

"*Very* British," I said.

Father returned soon enough. We sat on an Oriental rug or walked around, never far from the booth. People came and picked up brochures about the airlines and asked questions about rates and routes and supersavers and safety. I made Father bring me lunch because I didn't want to leave and miss Sabrina. She had not shown up all morning, and I did not intend to miss her when she did. I had a thing or two I wanted to show her, which was me in my striped burnoose. When Father arrived with my Big Mac, I pointed to my sandwich and said to the man from Mideast Airlines, "Very American. But the Japanese are going to miniaturize it and market it as the Mini-Mac. They're developing the transistors for it now."

He laughed, his gold teeth flashing, as in your basic adventure story.

My father laughed, too, and said to one of the swarthies, "It's a very clever boy I have." He looked at me with what is called approval.

Sabrina appeared around two. Lilly was carrying a shopping bag that said, "Go First Class. The First Class Travel Agency of Rahway, New Jersey."

"Well," I said to Sabrina, as nonchalant as you please, "What's new?"

"How do you pronounce *ts* in Pinyin?" she asked.

"What is Pinyin?"

"The new Chinese spelling. Obviously, if you don't know what Pinyin is, you don't know how to pronounce *ts* in it."

"I would say that's obvious, yes."

"Why do you want to know how to pronounce it?"

"Because of this." She pulled a newspaper clipping out of her pocket. There was a picture of a tall girl and a man standing on a stool with a tapemeasure. The caption said that the girl, who was sixteen years old, was seven feet, ten and a half inches tall, the world's tallest woman. Her name was Tseng Chin-uen.

"That's Pinyin all right," I said. "What do you think of me?" I asked, letting my hand sweep down the length of my burnoose.

"Eccentric," she said. "Very."

"Not around here, it isn't. Haven't you seen what's going on?"

"We just arrived. Actually, not just. We stopped by El Al, the Israeli Airlines. They were serving chicken soup for lunch."

"How was it? Was it gourmet?"

"It was authentic."

"But was it gourmet?"

"If chicken soup is gourmet, it's not authentic. Did you know that a recent study showed that chicken soup is good for the common cold?"

"Even if you're not Jewish?"

"Even if you don't have a cold."

"Do you have a banquet again tonight?" I asked.

"As a matter of fact we do."

"Father and I have to stay here until nine, when the displays close up. Will your banquet be over by then?"

"No, it will be in its middle," Sabrina said. "Ahmed looks just grand. How can you not like a camel that looks like that?"

"Borrowed finery," I said. "Will you have a banquet tomorrow night, too?"

"Yes. Big commercial conventions have a lot of banquets. Tomorrow night we've accepted an invitation to be the guests of the Spanish National Tourist Bureau. The Russian National Tourist Bureau is also having a banquet the same night, but everyone advised us that the food would be awful and the slide presentation would be all tombs and space shots. Spain, they say, is much sunnier."

"By the way, where is your mother's travel agency?"

"Lilly's travel agency?"

"Lilly, your mother."

Sabrina glanced over at her mother standing at the other end of the booth talking to Father.

"Rahway," she said, "Rahway, New Jersey."

"Is it First Class?"

"Of course it's first class. Small, but first class.

We always say that in Rahway to go first class, don't go First Class, go Lilly."

"What's the name of her place?"

She paused, sucked in her breath, and said, "Tours de Lilly."

"Will you come to the Exhibition Hall tomorrow?" I asked.

"I don't know. Mother wants me to go to some of the meetings with her. There are always so many meetings at a convention. So much to learn. All of our convention expenses are tax deductible, you know."

"Come by at noon tomorrow. I'll have a Big Mac waiting for you."

"Let me ask Mother."

Sabrina went over to her mother and pulled her away from Father. They conferred in whispers. Once or twice Sabrina held her hand to the side of her mouth so that I couldn't see her lips move. I saw Lilly looking over at me from time to time and nodding. Their conference seemed to me to take a long, long time. They seemed more like Watergate co-conspirators than like a daughter asking her mother for permission to have a Big Mac.

"Tomorrow, twelve-thirty," Sabrina said. Then she and her mother turned to leave. Lilly waved her hand, letting her fingers dance in the air.

I sat with two hamburgers, two fries and two shakes on my lap until the hamburgers were hard, the fries looked like they were coated with Vaseline, and the shakes looked like detergent foam after a batch of very dirty dishes. My feelings went from patience when she was fifteen minutes late, to impatience at thirty, to anger at an hour, to worry as suppertime came and went, and she still didn't show up.

Father said that there could be a hundred reasons why they didn't come. He gave me some change and told me to try calling them at their hotel. I tried once, then twice and returned to our booth each time. I thought that my best chance of finding them in their room would be just before suppertime when they were getting dressed for their banquet. Since it is not easy to use a phone in a loose burnoose and turban, I left them in the booth and walked outside the display area to where the telephones were, for I was determined not to leave until I got them. I kept trying, and finally Lilly answered the phone. "Oh, Maxwell," she said, "Sabrina was just asking me how we could get in touch with you. She's been so worried. Let me put her on."

I heard mumblings as the two of them had a conference while a hand was held over the telephone's mouthpiece. At last Sabrina was on the phone. She lost no time in apologizing. "Oh, Maximilian," she said, "I'm so sorry that we couldn't make it at twelve-thirty, but Mother had a very important business deal to discuss, and the man asked her to lunch, and he included me, and Mother felt it would look bad if I didn't go with her because she had rather insisted that he include me. She wanted me with her as sort of a chaperone, if you know what I mean. Have you ever had to chaperone your father?"

"Have I ever had to what?"

"You know, *be* there so that someone won't lay some heavy passes on your parent."

"No, I have never chaperoned my father, and—truth be told—I've never chaperoned my mother either."

"Maybe your mother, being more of a housewife, doesn't meet as many men as Lilly does being at conventions."

"My mother works. Not right now, of course, she's on her honeymoon, but she worked up until the wedding."

"Your mother got remarried?"

"Yes. She married F. Hugo Malatesta the First."

"The First? Are there others?"

"Two and Three."

"If he's a clone, that interests me."

"He's not a clone. He's a very rich man with a son who is the second F. Hugo, and a grandson, F. Hugo, who's the third."

"Well, congratulations," Sabrina said.

"For what?"

"For having a First stepfather."

"What do you mean by that?"

"Whatever you want it to mean."

"Will you be at the exhibition hall tomorrow?"

"I have to check with Lilly."

"I think you ought to come. These people pay hundreds and hundreds of dollars rent to put on displays for your pleasure and education. I'll introduce you to the dwarf who is playing a leprechaun."

"Okay, we'll be there. But don't count on me for lunch."

"The exhibits come down at two."

"See you tomorrow," she said.

I hung up and made my way back to the door into the exhibition floor, and the guard stopped me. I had left my badge pinned on my burnoose, and he would not allow me back in without it. I protested. I told him who I was, and he would not give in. I told him that I knew the names of the men at Mideast Airlines, that I knew the name of the camel-keeper and the name of the camel, but he would not give in.

Then I saw Maurice, one of the men in black tights who wore the dragon costume for Cathay Airlines. He was on his way out of the exhibit hall for a smoke. I asked him to please ask Father to bring me my burnoose with my badge. He said he would. Maurice tucked his cigarettes in his jersey sleeve and headed back inside the exhibition hall. Maurice was nice, but he had the look of someone who is doing something he doesn't want to do and who has been doing it a long time. The ninth-grade English teacher at Fortnum had more of that look than anyone else I've ever met. Maurice was a dancer by profession, and he said that he does gigs at conventions to earn his bread. A gig is a job, and he said he did gigs for the bread.

I had also talked to the chicken soup lady at El Al. Her name was Arabella Simpson. She told me that she was a pastry chef but what with everyone in the world worried about cholesterol, she had to give up on pastries and go into chicken soup. Jake Stone, the man who built the model of the Eiffel Tower, had started out his life as a sculptor. And Brumba, the African Safaritours man, was an actor who also did gigs at conventions to earn his daily bread. Only Scotty Devlin, the leprechaun, always worked conventions or side shows.

Father came to the door with my burnoose and my badge, and the guard let me in.

"Did you get Sabrina on the phone?" he asked.

"She'll stop by sometime tomorrow," I replied.

Father never asked why Sabrina had not stopped by, and I was glad he didn't. I didn't want him to get the notion that Lilly might want Sabrina to chaperone her when he was around. Of course, I'm not sure Father would get that notion, but I didn't want him to think it, and I wasn't sure why.

Ahmed emptied his bowels once while Father went out for our supper. I scooped it up, and circled around the room so that I could walk by the door where the guard who would not let me back in before was posted. As I passed him, I said, "The badge is under lumps one and two," and I walked on by. I carried it to the men's room and flushed it down, and I didn't even mention to Father about how helpful I'd been or about the shortcut I had discovered.

We were more tired that second night than we were after the first when we had done much more. Father said that it was always that way. That as far as he could tell, newness was the best vitamin pill in the world. We went to bed immediately after settling Ahmed.

The following morning I told Scotty Devlin that I had a friend who wanted to meet him. I told him even before I put on my burnoose. I twice approached the seven-foot man at the Air India Booth, but I didn't bother to introduce myself. Seven feet isn't so unusual. Not as unusual as three feet ten. To a basketball team, seven feet is almost basic. Besides, the man in the Air India Booth did not look at all talkative like Maurice or Scotty or Brumba. From where I stood he didn't even look friendly.

About a quarter to two Scotty, the Leprechaun, came over to our booth and said, "Where's your friend, Max?"

"She must have gotten detained," I answered.

"Well," Scotty said, "they paid me, so I'll be making my way out of here strictly at two."

"Sure," I said. "I understand."

At five minutes to two, Sabrina appeared in our booth without Lilly.

"Where's your mother?"

"She had to check us out of the hotel and load

up the car. We had a late lunch again. Mother didn't want me to come, but I insisted. I came only because I promised."

I saw that Father was consulting with the men from Mideast Airlines for our pay. I said to Sabrina, "Wait here. Let me see if I can catch Scotty." I started running toward the Irish Tourist Bureau booth. The man from Mideast called me and asked me to please return my burnoose and turban. I could understand his wanting me to. I could understand his thinking I was going to make off with them just as he was closing up shop. I could understand him. I really could. But I didn't have to like it. I saw Scotty just as he was waving goodbye to the Irish Tourist Bureau and walking out the service exit.

I ran back to our Mideast booth. Sabrina was sitting on the rolled rug. "You missed him," I said.

"I guess so," she said.

"Here was your one chance to meet a real freak, and you blew it."

"I guess I did," she said, "but I got to see Ahmed in all his finery. Aren't you glad that it's his now?"

"What's his?"

"That saddle. Those beautiful saddle bags. Everything belongs to Ahmed now and forever."

I looked over at the two swarthy men from Mideast. They were speaking to one another in a foreign language. I didn't understand what they were saying, but I knew that they were disagreeing about something. Disagreement is a universal language.

Sabrina pointed over her shoulder. "One of them thinks the other should have charged your father more."

"How much did they charge?"

"Five hundred," Sabrina said.

"But that's two days' pay for this gig," I said.

"It's this last day they're arguing about. The chief Arab over there says that your father should get only one hundred seventy-five for today since it was over at two o'clock, and your father says that he was promised two hundred fifty dollars for each of the days."

"How do you know which of those two swarthies is the chief Arab? I've been here two and a half days, and I don't know which is the more boss."

"Where did you say you went to school?"

"I didn't. I said I was going to go to Fortnum. You've never told me where you go. I don't even know where you're from."

"I told you, Maximilian. I told you that Tours de Lilly is in Rahway, New Jersey. And, naturally, I go to school there."

"How did school in Rahway teach you which one of these two was the chief Arab?"

She shrugged. "It's after school where I learn those things."

"What's going to happen? Will my father get two fifty or one seventy-five?"

Sabrina tossed a look over her shoulder and said, "They'll compromise at two hundred."

At that moment Father came toward us folding a check into his wallet. I would like to have been able to tell how much it said, but I could not, and I would not ask, for I was afraid that Sabrina would be right, and I did not mind her being right. I really didn't. I just minded her being terribly right.

Father said to Sabrina, "How did you get here?"

"Taxi."

He told her that with so many people leaving at once, it would be difficult to find a taxi, and he would drive her back to the Fairmont. So Sabrina came with us to the sub-basement where our truck was parked. Father unbridled Ahmed and laid the new saddle down in the back of the truck, in the end where the worse thing Ahmed could do would be to spit on it.

The three of us piled into the cab with Sabrina between Father and me. It was an awful ride. Because there was a question I wanted to ask Sabrina. I wanted to ask, but I didn't want to look as if I wanted to know the answer. So the ride to the Fairmont was short and silent. I realized that I would have to get down out of the truck to let Sabrina out. I thought that when I did so, I could walk her from the curb to the door of the hotel and ask her for her address and ask her if she would write back if I wrote first. I wanted to tell her that I would watch out for news of Renee. But once we pulled around the driveway, a doorman opened the door of the truck cab and I got down, reaching my hand up to help Sabrina. She stepped down, her hair bouncing once and twice, prettier than she had a right to be at her age and size. She turned, waved her hand once, then twice, and walked into the hotel. Another doorman held the door for her, and she gave him a half-nod, as practiced as an heiress in a basic adventure story. I saw Lilly waiting just inside the door.

We pulled out of the Fairmont's driveway, and Father said, "I guess you can get in touch with her at Tours de Lilly in Rahway, New Jersey."

"What makes you think I'm anxious to get in touch with her?"

"I thought that if you found out something about Renee, you might want to let her know."

There was no reason why my father, a man I hardly knew better than I knew F. Hugo Malatesta, should know what I was thinking. The fact that he did made me mad.

"How much money did you get for this last day's work?" I asked.

"We settled for two hundred," he said, "and Ahmed's old saddle."

I didn't say another word until Father asked me where I wanted to go for supper, and I said that I didn't care.

3

From Dallas we headed for Tulsa, Oklahoma. The Tulsa State Fair is held there in Expo Square. It appears that Father and Ahmed did the Fair every year. Father charged $1.00 for kids and $1.50 for adults for a four-minute ride on Ahmed. I don't know why he charged less for kids because it seemed to me that they were a lot more trouble, but I was not interested enough to ask. If you calculate that the Fair was open twelve hours a day and then calculate that he had a rider every four minutes (and allow one minute to load and unload the beast) and calculate that one rider every hour would be an adult, Father would make $150 a day, if we were kept busy every minute. The Fair lasted five days, so the most, the very, very most that Father could make at the Oklahoma Fair would be $750, which is less than it cost Mr. F. Hugo Malatesta to become a member of the dining club on top of the First Guaranty Bank Building in Philadelphia. But I didn't say anything.

I found out Father had paid booth rent in advance, and for that we also had the privilege of hooking our camper up on the fairgrounds.

We no sooner pulled into the fairgrounds and no sooner took Ahmed off the truck and tethered him to the hitch than a pack of kids came running over to Father calling, "Woody! Woody!" The smallest one made a running jump into his arms while the other three walked over to Ahmed and started stroking him and talking to him as if he were some kind of world-class animal.

Father lifted the one who had leaped at him high in the air. "How is my friend, Emmy?" Father asked. So it was a girl. All four of the kids looked alike: color-coded to mark them as a set; each one only slightly different in size. All except the smallest had boys' names: Manuelo, Iago, and—would you believe?—Jesus, pronounced Hay-soos. I wondered if he had gotten his name from some ancient Mexican Indian blindfold custom. I had to congratulate Father for being able to tell them apart when he introduced them to me one at a time.

"Wait until you see what I got," he said. He went to the truck and brought out Ahmed's new saddle and bridle. Those four kids each took a step back and looked afraid to touch it like it was some museum piece never to be touched instead of something to throw over a camel's back and sit on. The biggest of the four kids—who I thought was my age, but who I later found out was two years older—said, "Hey, Woody, did you keep the old one so that we can still ride?"

"No," Father said. "You still ride, but you ride the new saddle. Who's first?"

Emmy ricocheted out from a forest of legs and said, "Me! Me! Me!"

Manuelo not only saddled up Ahmed, he also helped Emmy get up, and then he led Ahmed around the paddock, tugging on the bridle, clicking his tongue and saying soft words. Whatever combination of things he did was right, for Ahmed didn't kick or spit. His stomach just rumbled, but nothing could stop that except a bullet to his brain.

Father leaned against the door of the camper and asked the middle boy, the one I would learn to distinguish as Iago, how was his mother.

"She's good. She didn't want to come this year. Said it was too much work. But we told her we wouldn't have no vacation at all if she didn't work the Fair. Emmy cried so much that Mama said her tears gonna make the tacos salty."

Father said to Iago, "Look, do you think you can unhitch Ahmed and settle him down for the night? I'm going to lie down for a few minutes." Father started into the camper and called out, "Say *hello* to your mamma for me."

Iago and Jesus waved and said, "Sure thing, Woody. She says the same to you."

I leaned against the wall of the camper, my arms folded across my chest, thinking Father could have asked me to settle Ahmed. So what if I didn't know how? He could have asked me instead of asking these strangers.

Iago asked me, "This your first time at the Fair?"

I nodded.

"We come every year," he said. "Our mama has a tacos stand." He pointed in a general direction. "They keep all the food stands together away from the animals. Mama's stand is called *Rosita's*. That's our mama's name. Our mama makes the best tacos at the Fair."

The littler one, Jesus, kept nodding the whole time the other was talking.

"Since you guys are going to close up shop, I'm going inside. You just put everything away, and I'll see you around. Okay?"

"You coming over to Rosita's for supper? Woody always has first night supper at our place. You come, too."

"I'll see," I said, and went into the camper.

Father was lying across my bunk, and I nudged him to ask him about supper. The minute I touched him, I felt that he was burning up. I pulled the blankets from the top bunk and covered him up and went back outside. Manuelo had just returned from leading Ahmed around the paddock. He commanded Ahmed to kneel, and Ahmed did so. He lifted Emmy from the saddle and said to Jesus, "You next."

I said to Iago, "I'm afraid my father has a fever. I think he's come down with the same bug I had about a week ago."

Emmy walked over to us. She reached for my hand and said, "I like the new saddle. Can I ride tomorrow?"

"I don't know," I said. "Woody is sick. I don't know. I just don't know."

Iago put his fingers in his mouth and made a whistle that a steam locomotive could have envied. When he did, Manuelo turned Ahmed around and cut across the center strip to make a beeline for us. "What's the problem?" he asked.

"Woody's sick."

Manuelo maneuvered Ahmed back into his kneeling position, and Jesus got off. He said to me, "I'll put Ahmed in his stall and feed him. I know where the stalls are. Iago, you take the others over to our place and stay with them and send Mama back here. Tell her that Woody's sick." Then he looked at me. "Don't worry, Max. You take care of Woody, and we take care of the rides. I can drive Ahmed as good as Woody can. Woody taught me hisself." He thought a minute and then added, "Unless you want to run the rides. I'll try to take care of Woody, but I'd be better at running the rides."

"If running Ahmed is your first choice, then you go right ahead and run Ahmed. I'll take care of Father."

"You get the sign and set it outside the camper.

I'll carry it on over to the track tomorrow morning."

"The sign?"

"Ahmed's sign. The advertising one that tells how much to pay."

"I don't know where Father keeps his sign."

"Under the table," he said.

"Oh. All right. I'll do that. I'll set it outside the camper tomorrow morning."

"That's right. Outside the camper. Here comes Mama," Manuelo said.

Down the field, across the worn-out pasture came Mama all right. She looked like the person for whom the word Mama was invented. She had Mama glands the size of cantaloupes and a stomach that started early and ended late. She was wearing blue jeans, and as she approached I saw that she had an advanced course of eye makeup on. Her hair was sprinkled with single gray hairs that announced themselves loud against all the other black ones. Her hair was parted in the middle and pulled straight back and held with a rubber band. When she turned around, you could see that her hair reached below her waist, even below the whole double mound of where she sat down.

"This is Max," Manuelo said.

She said, "Hi, Max," and asked me what was the matter, and I told her, and I also told her what I thought caused it. She sent Manuelo away, and the two of us went inside the camper. She reached across my bunk and felt Father's forehead. "Let's

67

get him undressed and sponge him down to bring the fever down," she said.

Mama Rosita was not at all embarrassed about undressing a helpless man. She was able to lift Father and sponge off his parts like he was a department store manikin that didn't have any. She put her hand back on his forehead. "That brought his fever down some," she said. "Do you think you can get him to take some liquids? Coke is good. And make sure when he takes aspirin, he takes a big glass of water. I'll send Manuelo over with some supper for you."

I told her thank you very much, but I wished that there were some words that meant one degree more. I wished there was a special vocabulary that said thanks when thanks are deserved and not even asked for.

Father did look pitiful. I stayed inside the camper making sure that he didn't get uncovered and take a chill. He was perspiring as if he'd been given a government franchise for it. When his breathing became regular, and I knew he was sleeping soundly, I began to look for the sign. I looked under the table but found nothing. I expected to find nothing because I had noticed nothing in all the time I had been staying with Father. I opened all the cabinets (two) and looked in them, and in the oven and even inside the half refrigerator, where I knew it wasn't. I found nothing. Then I decided to crawl under the table and feel around the floor boards and when I did, I looked up and saw that the actual underside of the kitchen table was painted, and the painting said:

BE A CAMEL RIDER
Ride AHMED
Children $1.00
Adults $1.50

The colors were sand, purple and red. I got out from under the table and saw that there were hinges connecting it to the camper wall and another hinge at the opposite end that dropped down to make the table leg. I loosened the pins and separated the hinges and had the sign ready for Manuelo.

He came with a bowl of chili that was a kind of spicy that was four beyond basic. I had to eat it slowly. Manuelo visited with me, and that's when I found out that he was two years older than I. I also found out that he had been working the Oklahoma State Fair for seven years.

"It's our vacation," he said.

"Vacation?" I asked.

"Yes, it wasn't too easy to get away this year. It keeps getting more expensive."

"Do you stay at a hotel?"

"What hotel? We stay in the camper. The front part is our taco and chili stand, and the back part is where we live."

"The five of you live in half a camper?"

"Yes."

"And the five of you work the taco stand?"

"Not Emmy. She's only five. She's too little to reach over from behind the counter."

"But you work?"

"Yes."

"May I ask you a question?"

"Okay."

"Why is it a vacation?"

"Because we're not picking melons and because it's fun. You get to do a lot of different things. Man! We meet people like Woody and Ahmed."

"Ahmed is not a people."

"But he is the only camel I've ever known. Where else would I get a chance to meet a camel?"

"At a shopping center. At a school fair. You could meet them there. They are not what you might call exclusive."

"It's a real sacrifice for our father to let us go."

"Which our father?" I asked, worried, considering the name of his second brother and considering that he'd said "sacrifice."

"Our father, Manuelo senior," he answered. "This is the height of the season."

"What season?"

"Melons. Cantaloupe mostly. We pick melons down in the Valley."

"What valley?"

"In Texas, the valley means the Rio Grande."

"This is Oklahoma."

"But we're from Texas, man. We vacation in Oklahoma."

Father spent what is called a restless night, and because he did, I did. A little bit of fever seemed to make him sleepy, but when his fever started to go up, he would waken, and I would give him Coke or ice water, or if enough time had passed, I would give him aspirin again. He looked feeble.

About six-thirty the next morning the sounds of the fairgrounds changed. Instead of an occasional animal noise and instead of the irregular creak of the seats of the ferris wheel and the eerie slap of the flag pole ropes against the pole as the wind blew them, I began to hear people. People calling to each other to say hello or to give an order. And the sounds of the animals changed from occasional to demanding. The sounds gathered together and got lost in noise the way a rainbow of clear colors gets lost to make white.

I slid down from the top bunk and did a quick job in what passed for a bathroom in Father's camper. I started out the door when I heard Father moan. It was not a very loud moan, but it was loud enough. I returned to his bunk.

"I've got to get up," he said. "I can't seem to find my senses. Would you please help me, Bo?"

"It's all right, Father," I said. "Ahmed is taken care of. Everything is all right. I think you should go back to sleep." It was not time for him to have aspirin again. Rosita had said two every four hours, so I held his head while he drank some ice water. He sank back down into the pillow. "Thanks, Bo," he said, and he fell asleep again.

I studied my father for the next few minutes, and besides deciding that I'd better not leave him regardless of how interesting the sounds outside became, I also decided that whatever it was that was making him sick sure wasn't stopping his hair from growing. Besides needing a shave, the hairs inside his nose and ears had sprouted like bread mold for a science project.

Mama Rosita came by about nine o'clock and asked about how Father was and how he had spent the night. She brought me some kind of donut that opened up and you poured honey in, and a cup of coffee. I would have preferred milk, but I was too polite to say so.

"I'm rushing back to the stand now," she said. "When the breakfast trade is all done, I'll be back to help you bathe Woody and change the sheets."

"I'm looking forward to it," I said, and she answered, "Good," and left.

After she left I sat down to eat the donut and drink the coffee, and I realized how lucky I am to be polite. It was a good thing I didn't tell her that I would have preferred milk because coffee went much better—just about perfect—with that kind of donut.

Mama Rosita returned about ten-thirty. Together we bathed Father. I wished we could shave him, too, but Mama Rosita said that appearances don't count, but that being clean does. Iago brought me lunch and later he brought me supper, and in between those times I cannot tell you what I did, but I was kept busy: taking the bottle to Father for him to empty his bladder or feeding him canned chicken soup or holding his head while he drank Coke or water. His fever seemed to go down after lunch, but it shot back up about four o'clock, and I kept sponging him off with cool wet washcloths.

When Iago brought me my supper about seven, I sat out on the camper step and asked him to join me, but he told me that he had to hurry back because he had to take Manuelo his supper, too, since they were short-handed in their booth. I ate alone there on the step, sniffing the air and deciding that although it was full of peculiar smells and particulates, it had a quality that sure *felt* healthy.

I heard a knock on the camper door about eleven. It was Manuelo. He laid a pile of bills on top of the counter, reached in his pocket for some change, and said, "Sixty-seven twenty-five. I kept ten bucks in bills and coins to make change."

"How can you have twenty-five cents? I thought the rides were a dollar or a dollar fifty. The money should be in multiples of fifty cents."

"You thinking I cheated you?"

"I was just . . ."

"The truth is that you were cheated."

"I didn't mean . . ."

"But I didn't cheat you. Some gringo accused me of giving him wrong change, and I made it up to him even though I'm not at fault. In this business, man, you learn not to fight over two bits. You lose good will to fight in front of the customers."

"Listen, Manuelo, I didn't mean for you to think that . . ."

"You didn't mean for me to think what, man?"

"I didn't mean for you to think that I thought you were cheating."

"Sure, man."

"It's just that I have this rather good ability in math."

"Sure, man."

"Listen, Manuelo . . ."

"No, you listen," he said. "I'm not sure I like you, but I'll tell you this. I love Woody. And so does Mama and Iago and Jesus and Emmy, too. We've loved him all the years we been coming to Tulsa. And we gonna continue to do for you because we're really doing for Woody, and we're not gonna let him down." He picked up my supper dishes. "I'll take these back to Mama. You tell Woody that Ahmed was a good boy today, and he's all settled for the night."

"I'll tell him," I said. "And would you please tell Mama Rosita thanks for the supper? Would you tell her that I said it was real good." He turned to leave. "Would you also please tell her that?"

"I'll tell her," he said and left.

After he left I told myself that Manuelo was just pretty touchy and shouldn't have jumped to any conclusions, and I told myself it was not my fault if I was rapid-fire in arithmetic, and after he left I hated him. Or me. I guess it was me I hated, but I hated him for making me.

Father's fever broke that night, and by morning he awoke smiling and talked about getting up and getting going. I let him try, but, of course, he couldn't. He sat halfway up and sank back down. "I'm as weak as May wine," he said.

"Just lie there," I said. "Would you like to have solid food today?"

"No, Bo," he said. "I don't feel strong enough to chew."

"How about a mashed potato?"

"No, thanks," he said. And he was asleep again in five seconds.

Mama Rosita appeared again, and I told her that Father's health seemed to be improving, and she told me that it was time to change the sheets, and I told her that I couldn't find any more clean ones, and I didn't know what we would be changing them to, and she told me that she would send Iago over to baby-sit with Father and that I should take the sheets to the laundromat and wash them. I told her sure. I didn't have any idea how to do laundry. I didn't explain that laundry was one of the services we got for living on the Fortnum campus, and she

75

didn't ask. I wished she would have asked, but she didn't. She just asked me if I had quarters, and I told her that I did, that Manuelo had given them to me, and I looked at her out of the corner of my eye so that I could see if she would give any hint about whether Manuelo had said anything to her about the money. But there was no hint, so I didn't know if he didn't say anything or if she just made it look as if he hadn't.

Iago came with Emmy. He didn't act as if Manuelo had said anything to him either.

I gathered together all the dirty clothes that we had and wrapped them in a sheet. Emmy then went to the cupboard and got a box of detergent and handed it to me. I started out the door. Emmy called after me. "Wait for me. I'm sposed to take you."

I thought that lugging a couple weeks' supply of dirty clothes including an extra set of sheets plus a box of detergent was enough to do without baby-sitting, too. But Emmy came along. She reached up for my hand that I thought I needed to help support the load I had slung over my shoulder. She took me straight to the laundromat. The minute that I set the bundle of sheets down, she began sorting them according to some system that I had seen but never taken seriously on television commercials. She then looked over the four piles and lumped two of them together. "We won't use bleach this week," she said, "and we'll use the heavy loaders." Then she asked me for nine quarters, which I gave her. She filled three washing machines, standing on a step stool that was nearby. She put three quarters, one after the other, in each of the three slots and came over to the row of chairs where I was sitting. She climbed into a chair next to me, turned, crossed her arms across her chest and said, "Let's hope none of these suckers break down. The mother who runs this place screams and won't give you your money back when they do."

I scratched my head and said nothing. Emmy continued to sit there, her arms folded across her chest, staring at the washers while they filled up and began doing whatever it is they do.

"You can go home," I said. "I'll wait."

"Mama told me to help."

"Did Manuelo say anything to your mama about me?" I asked.

"About your checking on the money, you mean?"

"Well, about that or about anything else."

"Manuelo just said that you're a asshole, and Mama, she said that you're young for your age and that we should remember that what we do is because we love your papa. No one said anything else. Jesus looked like he wanted to say something, but Mama told him to zip up and get to bed."

We sat in silence until the machines finished their cycle, and then Emmy showed me how to dry the clothes and fold them when they were done. On the way back to the camper, she held my hand again just like someone who is really her own age.

That night when Manuelo stopped by with the money, he just put it down on the counter. I said nothing, and he said nothing. Mama Rosita and Iago, or Jesus or Emmy came by at times during the day, and so did a lot of the Fair regulars. They brought gifts for Father. A man who had a hot dog concession brought a six-pack of beer. Two Indians from the Five Civilized Tribes Booth of Indian Folk Art brought Father a blanket from all of them. (It was a large booth.) Pete, a security guard, brought a cellophane pack of Tom's cheese crackers. Fanny brought a basket of fruit from all of the game concession people. I had to thank each of them and give each a health report on Father. I now knew why when famous people get sick, they have a hospital spokesman give health bulletins at certain times during the day. I got tired of saying that Father had had a good night or that his fever was down. I got tired of saying the same things, and I got tired of hearing the same things. *So you're Bo? How do you like our Fair? That's some nice guy you have for a daddy. You take good care of that old man now, hear?*

I got tired of it all.

I got tired of hearing how Father was one of the nicest guys in the world.

On the last day of the Fair, Father was feeling well enough to get dressed and shaved and sit for short periods of time on the camper step. "Hey, Bo," he said, "why don't you take a day off and just wander around the fairgrounds and see what there is to see. I'll be all right." He reached inside his pocket and handed me ten dollars. I told him I didn't want it. "Aw, go on," he urged.

"I don't want pay for my services," I said. "I have fifty dollars that Mr. Malatesta gave me."

Father put the ten back in his pocket. "Have it your way." He shrugged.

"And now that you're fully conscious, I would appreciate being called Maximilian."

I walked away. I don't know why I said that to Father. I really didn't mind being called Bo. When people have names as strange as Jesus, it doesn't much matter if you're called Bo instead of Maximilian or Max.

Father told me that he was going over to the track to see Ahmed, and he invited me to come along, but I didn't.

The sounds of the fairground were different that night. Everyone was breaking up camp, doing as much repacking as they could so that they could pull out early in the morning. Manuelo came by with the sign and the money. He told Father that he had locked the gear in the box in the truck, and he also told him that he was glad that he was feeling better.

I was anxious to see how Father would handle this thank you because it was a big one. This is what

Father did: he punched Manuelo in the upper arm. It was what is called an *affectionate* punch, and he said, "Manuelo, whenever you want a job, you have one with me if you can find me."

Manuelo said, "Sure, Woody, and whenever you want the best tacos in Texas, you can buy them at Mama Rosita's at a discount." Then he gave Father a light jab in the stomach.

"Now you wouldn't dare try that if I were a healthy man."

"No. Then it would be full of tacos."

"I'm coming with you to your mama's. I want to say goodbye until next year."

Neither invited me to go along, so I didn't.

Manuelo and Father left with the air between Manuelo and me still ugly enough to give cramps. I made certain that I was in bed before Father got back. I was glad that Father's illness had made me move to the upper bunk because that way he didn't have to see me when he came back. He took his old guitar down and started strumming and humming. I called down from my bunk, "I thought you said that we'd have a long drive tomorrow. Don't you think you ought to get some sleep?"

"I've been sleeping a lot, Bo."

I climbed down out of my top bunk. I had to know. "Did Manuelo say anything to you about me?"

"No. Should he have?"

"I just wondered if he mentioned anything about the money?"

Father said no, and then I told him what had happened. He said nothing. He said nothing for a long time. He just kept his hands on his guitar and continued to say nothing until finally I said, "Aren't you going to say anything?"

"Next time don't be so anxious to show how smart you are."

"That's next time. What can I do about Manuelo?"

"Nothing. Except consider it a lesson for next time."

"You sure don't know anything about how to comfort someone."

Father started strumming his guitar again. I waited. If Father could be good at saying nothing, I could be better at waiting. He stopped strumming, but he didn't put his guitar down. He did look up at me and study me for a long, long time. I waited that out, too. At last he said, "Tell me, Bo, if you had your first choice of anything in the world to do for the rest of this month, what would it be?"

"I'd be on that cruise with Mother and F. Hugo Malatesta the First. I'd be eating in the first-class dining room and I'd be strolling around the first-class deck and I'd be swimming in the first-class pool."

"Would you feel more at home there than you do here?"

"I don't know if I would. How should I know if I would? All I know is that first class is something I was meant to get used to, and life with a camel isn't any kind of training for it."

Father laughed. He put his guitar down and said, "Come here, Bo." I hesitated. He repeated, "Come here." I did.

He put one arm around me and then the other. "Do you know what? I would like to be on that cruise, too. I would like to be going first class. And do you know why? Not because it's something I want to get in practice for but because I'd like to watch those people. It would be like watching people from another country. And then ever afterwards, I'd know that I had seen something up close that I'd never seen before." He pushed me away from him, just a little way. Our eyes were on the same level. He said, "Let me ask you this, Bo. Do you think you could visit with me, with Ahmed, as I would visit that cruise? Like a foreigner? Watching the customs and saying, 'Oh, that's strange. Oh, that's new'—but remembering that you're a visitor, and visitors don't set the customs; they observe them. Do you think you could do that?"

"Sure. I could do that," I said. "But you're asking me to try to be something I'm not."

"How do you know that Mr. Malatesta isn't asking the same thing?"

I thought about that awhile before I realized that I didn't really know what Mr. Malatesta was asking. Father pulled me toward him. It was a hug.

"I'll do it," I said. He tightened his hold on me. "There's just one thing more I want to say."

"What's that?"

"I'm really sorry about Manuelo."

"I know, Bo. I know you are. You probably will be for a long time."

"And I really don't like camels."

"That's two things, Bo; that's two things."

We went to bed, and I felt ready to be a stowaway in Father's summer. I even felt a little anxious to.

Our next stop was Oakes' Dude Ranch outside Denver. We took two days getting there. Father's strength was at about three-fourths, and remembering how the disease had wiped me out, I could tell that he was pushing it, so I made up a few extra hunger pangs and a few extra calls of nature that I described as urgent. Father never suspected what I was doing and never got impatient with me for doing it.

Father said that I would like Oakes. It was a big place where conventions brought people by the busload for an evening's or an afternoon's entertainment. They had a big ranch meal with steaks grilled on the outdoor grills. In the evening some of the ranch hands would sing around a campfire. And the people would ride horses. Father had been bringing Ahmed for the past five years because being that there were more Eastern city folk at these conventions than almost anything else, they felt awkward about riding horses. But since no one knew how to ride a camel and everyone looked awkward doing it, Ahmed had been a big hit, and they had invited Father back year after year. We would be eating with the conventioneers, he said. Gave them a better feeling to be eating with the ranch hands. They thought it was more authentic, and it gave them a chance to talk to someone who didn't do the same daily things they did. The ranch hands all doubled at waiting tables plus something else: like singing or helping people on the horses or doing rope tricks.

"Conventions are funny things, Bo," he said. Father had taken to calling me Bo all the time now, and I hardly reminded him about it anymore. Actually, I had altogether stopped reminding him.

"Conventions are a way of life," he said.

Sabrina had said the same thing.

"Everyone comes together united by something. They're all doctors or they're all doctors of cancer or they're all doctors of cancer of the pancreas. Or the liver or the esophagus. But, here's the funny thing about the people. I've never seen them at their meetings, but they never talk about what it is that unites them when they're not at a meeting. Houses. They talk a lot about houses and the cost of them. And the stock market. And the cost of stocks. That's what they talk about mainly: what things cost.

"We'll have good meals, but it will be the same thing every time. The people will be different.

There are certain types that always show up at any convention, and you'll get to meet some of each type."

We plugged in at the ranch about noon. Father unleashed and fed Ahmed while I made sandwiches for lunch. Then we drove into town and Father bought me two western shirts and two bandannas for around my neck. I already had jeans. I decided to buy boots with part of the money Mr. Malatesta had given me. I discovered that the boots I really wanted took all of it. Father said, why not? And I said that meant the boots were worth fifty kiddy rides on Ahmed, and Father said, so what? And so I bought them. After all, I had promised Mr. Malatesta to spend the fifty dollars foolishly, and boots didn't seem foolish unless they were expensive, and I explained my thinking to Father.

He didn't agree. "To buy fancy and expensive boots is not foolish, but talking about it is."

I understood what he meant.

We got back to the dude ranch before the first bus of conventioneers arrived from town. Father introduced me (as Bo) to the people who worked at the ranch. One of them was Ruth Britten, and she seemed more glad to see Father than any of the others. I watched her a lot. The first convention group that came were social workers, and I have never seen a more sincere bunch of people. Ruthie Britten asked one man if he would like another cup of coffee. He did not say, "Yes, thank you" or "No thanks," he said, "How kind of you to ask," and then he turned to the person sitting next to him and asked, "How do you feel about another cup of coffee, Sam?" And Sam said, "Do you think it's decaffeinated?" and the first man said, "Good question. Shall we ask?" Sam said, "I suppose we should." The first man turned to Ruthie, who was standing there holding the coffeepot, and asked, "May I ask, please, is the coffee decaffeinated?" and she said, "No, it isn't, but I'll speak to the management about it. You decaffeinated drinkers need more representation." The man smiled at her and then smiled at his friend and said, "That's true. This young lady has made a good point." Then Ruthie Britten lifted her coffeepot and said, "How about it, boys? Feeling brave?" They both nodded and took seconds.

I liked that Ruthie Britten, and on the way back to the camper that night, I told Father about how she had handled those two men. "What's she do besides wait on tables?"

"She drives the bus to Denver to pick them up. She's smart all right," Father said. "She's a school librarian down in Lafayette, Louisiana, the rest of the year. She works here summers during the height of the convention season. We've been meeting at Oakes' Ranch for about four years now. Tonight will start our fifth."

"Tonight?"

"Yes," Father said. We were back at our camper now, and he was pulling his shaving things from out of the closet. He put them into a little zipper kit that I didn't even know he owned. He took out a fresh shirt and a change of underwear, too. He said as he started toward the door, "Better set the alarm. Breakfast is at seven down at the ranch house. Allow yourself fifteen minutes to walk there. See you in the morning."

"Well!" I said, "you sure seem to have recovered from your illness in a hurry."

"Thanks to your fine care."

"Care!" I said. "Care is something you seem to know nothing about. You don't even *care* if I'm left all alone in a strange land with not even a telephone to call on."

"Ruthie's camper is just four down—on the left. You won't even have to call very loud."

"Mother didn't send me halfway across the Continental USA to spend a month with you only to be abandoned."

Father shrugged. "I'm spending this night and all the nights that we're at Oakes' Ranch at Ruthie's. Now if you want to make a complaint of child neglect, you just take a bus into Denver and catch that convention of social workers. They're all good listeners, and they'll like your story."

"What if there's an accident and the camper catches on fire?"

"Don't play with matches," Father said. "See you at breakfast."

I didn't have to set the alarm, for Father knocked my door at six-thirty. "Better get up, Bo," he said.

I looked out the window, and there was Ruthie Britten standing next to Father, looking all clean and scrubbed in her blue jeans and plaid shirt, waving to me like a basic television sit-com mother. She wasn't young. She wasn't as young as Mother. And she wasn't pretty. She wasn't as pretty as Mother. And she had fat thighs.

"Hurry up, now, hear?" she called. "We'll wait for you, and we'll walk on over together." Ruthie had a definite Southern accent.

"I'm not hungry," I said.

"We are," Father said, and he put his arm around Ruthie's waist and started to turn her toward the ranch house.

"All right!" I called. "I'll come."

I dressed in a hurry. My jeans, one of my new shirts, my boots, and my navy blazer.

We sat at long tables for breakfast, and the talk was mostly of what the schedule was for the day and about pro football, which had started its demonstration games. I was the only non-adult there, but I don't think these people would have changed their descriptions of things if I had been a girl non-adult instead of a boy. I listened for a good time and calculated that if you took four adjectives out of their vocabularies, you would cut their descriptions down to nothing. It's easy to guess three of the adjectives; the fourth is hyphenated.

Everyone carried his plate with him from the table and stacked it on a counter in the back of the room. There they all spread out in the directions they needed to do their chores for the day. Father headed toward Ahmed, and Ruthie Britten headed toward the kitchen. Father gave her a squeeze around the neck before they went their separate ways.

No one invited me to go one way or another, and I pretty much didn't know what to do with myself. I suppose that in my Fortnum blazer I didn't look ready to work in either the kitchen or the stable. I suppose that if I had volunteered to help someone with the horses or with the food, they would have accepted my offer. But I didn't see any reason to offer my services to anyone. I stuck to my part of the bargain and acted like a visitor to a foreign country. I found a newspaper lying on one of the tables. I picked it up and carried it with me back to the camper. Since I had the whole morning with nothing to do, I did a thorough job of reading it after I took off my jacket. It was the day that the paper ran the ads for the grocery stores, and since they had to print enough news to fit the spaces in between the ads, there was a lot to read.

One of the articles was about Renee. With a

picture. It showed Renee holding up a bandaged hand. The article said that they still had not caught the person who had pushed her, and they still didn't know how much use she would have of her hand.

I cut that article out of the paper immediately after memorizing it, and I wrote the date at the top, and I would have embedded it in plastic if I had plastic and if I had known how to embed things in plastic when you had it. I put it in an envelope instead and sealed the envelope and put it in the breast pocket of my blazer right under the Fortnum crest. I laid my blazer across the bed carefully so that the clipping wouldn't wrinkle or fall out. I decided to write Sabrina something very clever as soon as I thought of it.

Father came for me about eleven-thirty. He said that the Oakes' Ranch would be receiving two busloads of Lambda Gammas for lunch and an afternoon of fun and games. I thought that Lambda Gammas were South American beasts of burden, but he told me that Lambda Gammas, who called themselves LG's, were a sorority. Fun and games meant that the rodeo riders would do demonstrations of roping and tying for anyone who cared to watch.

"What will Ahmed do?" I asked.

"He will be available," Father answered. "How about coming on over to the ranch house and helping to set up? They'll have to get this group fed and entertained and everything cleared away before the next batch arrives for supper."

"I have some correspondence to do before the evening group comes. I'll have to give it to someone to take into Denver to general delivery." General delivery was where Father had picked up his mail in Dallas and in Tulsa.

"The mail comes here, too, Bo. It's one of my standard summer mail stops." They deliver it once a day, and they pick up anything that needs to be mailed.

"I guess my letter can wait," I said. The truth was that I had not yet thought of something clever to say to Sabrina. I reached for my blazer, remembered the clipping, and decided not to wear it. It was getting warm outside anyway.

The buses arrived, and almost everyone who got off was a woman. About one out of three of the women had a child with her. About three out of the four children were girls. And one of them was Sabrina Pacsek.

I didn't know whether I should run back to the camper to get the clipping, or run to meet Sabrina. Before I could even make a decision, my new boots had carried me halfway across the pasture, and my hands were up in the air, yelling, "Sabrina! Sabrina!" And she heard me.

She waved back and said, "Hi, Max, what are you doing here?"

Before I could catch my breath I told her. She

was wearing jeans, a plaid shirt and a chino kind of jacket. She took the jacket off, folded it so that the lining was outside and slung it over her arm.

"Where's your mother?" I asked.

"Right over there," she said.

I looked to where she was pointing, and there I saw a woman who—except for the bare fact that she looked exactly like Lilly Pacsek—didn't resemble her at all. She no longer had the wife-of-the-delegate hairdo; she had her hair cut just below her ears, and it was held in place by a single barrette. It was blonde, sprinkled with careless gray. She was not wearing a pants suit or blue chiffon; she was wearing a plaid cotton skirt, a cotton tee shirt and a button-down navy blue sweater. Lilly Pacsek looked exactly like all the Fortnum School mothers except my own. In Havemyer, it's called preppy.

"What are you doing here?" I asked.

"We're attending the convention of Lambda Gammas."

"But I thought your mother is a travel agent. How can you be a Lambda *and* a travel agent?"

"The same way you can be a Southern Baptist and a travel agent or a Rotarian and a travel agent. What you do has nothing to do with it. Lambda Gammas are a college sorority, and they have a convention every other year to get together to discuss their goals. And all their goals are social and charitable."

"Where did you convene last time?"

"Mother and I didn't attend last time."

Something was wrong with Sabrina's answers, but I couldn't tell exactly what, so I didn't say anything.

"How are Ahmed and Woodrow?" she asked.

"They're both fine now," I said. "And so is Renee. I got a clipping from this morning's paper that shows her picture and her bandage."

"Yes, I have it," she said.

"You mean you don't want mine?"

"I never collect duplicates. Definitely no. Duplicates and freaks are a contradiction of terms."

I thought about that a minute, and I decided that she was right.

Lilly came over toward us and greeted me. She shook my hand with enthusiasm. And even before she finished pumping on my hand, Sabrina asked her mother if she couldn't help her off with her sweater since it seemed so warm at the ranch. "It's all right, dear," Lilly said. "It's still cool in the shade."

"Here, let me help you off with it," Sabrina insisted and then, instead of standing behind her mother, stood in front of her and began tugging at the sweater to pull it off. Lilly was saying, "Sabrina, dear, it's all right! I'm really not too warm." But Sabrina persisted and got that sweater off her mother's back and folded it inside out and handed it back to her mother. Lilly was wearing a sleeveless tee shirt, and there in the high, thin air of Denver,

Lilly stood with her arms folded across her chest, her hands rubbing the goose bumps of her upper arms. Sabrina was trying to hide their HELLO tags, and I made up my mind to find out why. I decided to sit between the two of them at lunch. It would give me a better chance to see one tag or the other and I wouldn't mind sitting next to Sabrina anyway.

"Is Woodrow here?" Lilly asked.

"He's here. If you find a waitress named Ruthie Britten, you'll find him right nearby."

"Is Ruthie Britten a good friend of his?"

"A *close* one," I answered.

Father found us and asked Lilly to save him a space on the bench near her, and Lilly did by putting her pocketbook down on the bench to her right and laying her sweater over the top of it. I sat on the other side of that space saver. I was determined to see Lilly's HELLO badge. Lilly was talking to the woman on her left and saying, "It's all right. These things happen."

The woman, who had the same hairstyle as Lilly and the same way of dressing, began telling Lilly a story about when she and her husband—may he rest in peace—had arrived in Karachi, Pakistan, for a convention of computer specialists and they had had no record of their reservations. No record at all. And her husband had had to call the American Embassy to find them a place to stay and they couldn't find them a place to stay either, and so they spent the night at the Embassy itself. "And, my dear, let me tell you, the accommodations were so fantastic that I was tempted to do the same thing the following year when we were scheduled for a conference in Algiers. But, of course, I did not. A person can only pull that sort of thing off once in a lifetime."

"Yes," Lilly answered. "Thank goodness, our problem was much simpler."

Sabrina saw that I was listening to her mother's conversation, so she nudged me with her elbow and said, "Did you know that the Crisco Kid died?"

"The Crisco Kid?"

"Yes. He was ten. He had a rare skin disease called *epidermolysis bullosa.* Made blisters form all over him. Even his tongue. And webs grew between his fingers and toes. They had to paint him twice a day with Crisco. Was the only thing he got relief from. That's how he got his name, the Crisco Kid."

"How do you catch epiderm . . . whatever?"

"By having the wrong parents. You inherit it from them."

"Did he die of it?"

"No, he died of a heart attack."

"Don't you think that having this epidermolysis stuff helped?"

"Oh, sure. Just as having Cockayne's disease helped Penny die of chicken pox."

"You've got it backwards," I said. "The chicken pox and the heart attack helped Penny and the

Crisco Kid die of their own special diseases."

Sabrina studied me a long time and then said, "Maximilian, what you don't seem to understand is that once you're a freak, a born one or a man-made one, anything you do that's normal becomes freakish."

"By your logic, then, anything freakish that a freak does is normal."

"Sure. Now, you take David."

"I know a lot of Davids. Which David?"

"The boy in the bubble in Houston. His name is David. The family won't reveal his last name. He has something wrong with him so that his body cannot fight germs, so he lives in a room-sized container where air is pumped in and germs are kept out. If you were to sneeze at David, you could kill him. He's nine years old now, and the only reason he has reached the age of nine is that he's never tried to be normal. He's never tried to be anything but a freak."

"But Renee was not born defective. She's the victim of an accident. She can still live a normal life."

"I wouldn't call it *normal*."

"She can overcome what happened to her."

"Overcoming is not normal. Overcoming means always having to do that plus whatever else she wants to do. It's like she will always have to put something on before she puts on her clothes."

"She always *will* have to put something on before she puts on her clothes. It's called underwear. Unless you want to tell me that girls don't wear underwear, and judging from what I've seen on television and in my mother's trousseau, I would say that they do, and I'd also say it's pretty expensive."

Sabrina did not blush. I had hoped she would, but would have been disappointed if she had. She said, "*Overcoming* is not like putting on underwear before you put on your clothes. It's like putting on a suit of armor before you put on your clothes. Everything you wear takes the shape of the armor."

"I'd say that makes it basically hard to relax."

"And to pretend."

"Why would anyone want to pretend?" I asked.

"Everyone wants to pretend sometime. Needs to. But freaks like David who lives in a bubble or the Crisco Kid or Renee cannot. They cannot live with disguises. Only normal people like you and me and Lilly and Woody have any choice about whether or not we want to present ourselves or present a disguise."

I thought about what she said, and although I agreed with most of it, I couldn't agree with all of it. "Woody is always Woody," I said. "He doesn't seem to fit in anywhere exactly. He's an exception, I think. Woody doesn't pretend about anything to anyone."

"I don't believe that," Sabrina said.

"How could you know? You hardly know my

father. You've seen him only . . ."

"I don't have to know Woody exactly. I know people."

"I thought your big specialty was freaks."

"I know freaks from having read about them. I know people from having been around, and I can tell you, Maximilian Stubbs, that when you really get to know your father, you're going to find that he's got disguises. Everyone does. I'm telling you, Max, only freaks have to live without disguises."

"How old are you?" I asked.

"My chronological age is ten," she answered. "But that is merely one of my disguises."

Father was approaching, and Lilly waved to him to show him where we were. I lifted Lilly's pocketbook and sweater from the bench between us. I saw her HELLO tag. It said: HELLO, I'M Lilly Walker, University of Michigan, 1958.

Father sat down and greeted Sabrina and Lilly warmly, and Ruthie Britten sat down directly across from Sabrina and studied her and asked the questions. "How do you like Denver?" "It's lovely." "What grade are you in?" "Going into fifth." "What do you think you would like to be when you're grown up?" "A plastic surgeon." "Where did you come from?" "Salt Lake City."

"I thought you came from Rahway, New Jersey," I said.

"That's where I live and go to school, but I just came from Salt Lake City."

"And," I said, thrusting her mother's HELLO badge in her face, "your name is Pacsek; here it says *Walker*."

"Mother has resumed her maiden name. Said it gave her a better sense of self."

"How could she do that if you're from Rahway?"

"The legal papers came through while we were visiting Salt Lake City."

I reached across her lap and picked up her sweater. Her HELLO badge said, *Sabrina Walker*. "Did you have your name changed, too?"

"No. I just called myself that for this convention. It makes it much easier for mother to introduce me by the same name she has."

There was something wrong. I knew that anyone with my mathematical abilities should be able to figure out what it was. I thought a minute and it came to me, clear as the answer to one plus one. "You mean to tell me that you are going around announcing yourself as Sabrina Walker, daughter of Lilly Walker?" She nodded. "And Walker was your mother's unmarried name?"

"Yes, when she was a Lambda Gamma at Michigan, she was known as Lilly Walker."

"That means that you are saying that you are your mother's daughter, and your mother is using her unmarried name. Do you know what that makes you?"

Sabrina stared at me a long time. Her eyes looking straight at me, then through me. At last she said, "Maximilian Stubbs, of all the ways there are to be smart in this world, I never want to be smart like you."

"Maybe I can't help being smart."

"Your trouble, Maximilian, is that you're not so smart that you're a freak about it, and you're not smart enough to pretend."

We ate in silence for a while, and one of the girls from down at the end of another table came over. "We're done," the girl said. "Our table got served first." Both Sabrina and I looked at her and said nothing. "We're done," she repeated, looking at me.

Sabrina said, "This young lady is Jennifer Susan Anderson. She has not one but two of the most popular names in the fifth grade." Jennifer Susan smiled. "But since she's from Begonia, South Carolina, she is known by one and all as Jenny Sue."

"Pleased to meet you, Jenny Sue," I said.

"What's your name?" she asked.

"My name is Maximilian Stubbs. Most people around here call me Bo."

"Max's father owns the camel, Ahmed. Maybe you'd like to look at Ahmed and take a ride on him."

Jenny Sue asked where he was; I pointed in some general direction, and Jenny Sue started skipping off. "I'll get there first," she said.

After she was out of earshot, Sabrina said, "A head cold is more interesting than that child." Then she raised her eyebrows and said to me, "I didn't know you had a nickname."

"I don't like it."

"Why did you tell us then?"

"I thought that Jenny Sue, being a South Carolina sorority girl, would appreciate it. Bo sounds sort of Southern."

Sabrina said, "I find that interesting."

"What do you find interesting?"

"What you choose to try to fit into."

Sabrina walked with me over to the riding track, and we watched Ahmed while others took rides. Three times I asked Sabrina if she would like to ride him. She said no three times. "I thought you liked Ahmed," I said.

"I do, but I don't care to ride him. I like the *idea* of a camel. I mean that I'm awfully glad there are camels in this world."

"Why?"

"Because they are strange. And I'm awfully glad I got to know someone who owns one."

"Why?"

"Because he has a strange son."

I had never thought of myself as strange; I can honestly say that I have spent all my time that I can remember trying not to be strange. Trying to be as normal as everyone else at Fortnum Preparatory School for Boys. I thought about Sabrina a lot that night. I had a lot of time to think about her. Father was at Ruthie Britten's again. He had taken his guitar.

We stayed at Oakes' Dude Ranch for ten days, and I had a lot of time to think. When we were ready to move on to Las Vegas, I knew two things: I still did not like camels, and I liked Sabrina. And looks had nothing to do with either. Maybe looks had nothing to do with either.

5

On our way to Las Vegas Father told me that he was especially glad to have Ahmed's new livery because in Las Vegas, Ahmed would be in show business. Ahmed had been hired by the Pyramid Hotel to star in their revue called "Arabian Chic," and the star of the show would ride on stage on top of Ahmed. Rehearsals would begin the day after we got there, and Father would be doing this gig—two shows a night—for three months.

"I'm sorry you won't get to see Ahmed perform," he said. "But minors are not allowed."

"Can I watch the rehearsals? I asked.

"I'll check and see," Father said.

After we settled Ahmed at the trailer park, we had a whole day to explore Las Vegas, and this is the way I would describe it: On the edge of the desert there is a highway with restaurants, gambling parlors and hotels on both sides. All of the hotels have many restaurants, many theaters and a large gambling casino on the inside. All of them have bright lights on the outside. This row of hotels is called "The Strip." And what it is most like is a comic strip. One section follows another, and all are more or less the same things drawn differently. Everything has stronger outlines and brighter colors than what is real. And within The Strip there are no real conversations, just words in balloons. And the guys who use The Strip do not have to think, but the people who invent it do.

The next day we drove to the Pyramid Hotel and entered a parking area below ground. We parked the truck and then we parked Ahmed. We took him from the truck and tethered him between the support pillars of the garage. We found a metal door that led up a short flight of stairs.

"The back door again," I said to Father.

"This time it's the stage door, Max. We're in show business."

There was so much confusion backstage that no one paid any attention to the fact that I, an under-legal-age boy, was helping out. Father never bothered to check with anyone to see if I was allowed to. Backstage I had expected to see girls who looked like cosmetic commercials, but instead I saw girls who looked like you could put a grocery cart in front of them and turn them loose in a grocery store, and even the meat manager wouldn't turn his head.

Father said, "Wait until they put on their glamor outfits for evening."

"But you said I wouldn't be allowed in this evening."

"You probably won't be. Some of the girls will be topless."

"I saw a girl nursing her baby right in your trailer park right in Smilax, Texas."

"Not the same thing," Father said.

"Why not?"

"Because no one was charging admission."

"Will the girl riding Ahmed be topless?"

"No. The star of the show is never topless."

"Who's the star of the show?"

"Trina Rose. She's an old friend of mine. Of your mother's, too."

"You mean Trina Rose, the English singer? The one who recorded *Walkin' Papers?*"

"Yes."

"And *Cry for Baby Love?* And *Home Neat Home?*"

"Yes, that one."

"Mother never told me she was a friend of Trina Rose's."

"Maybe it didn't seem important to your mother."

"When did you meet her?"

"Back when I lived at the ranch outside Taos. Trina Rose was known as Baby Bloom then. Her real name is Catarina Rosenblum, but she came to the ranch as Baby Bloom. She was just one of the dozens of kids who came around with a guitar and crashed at my place. That was before she hit it big. When she heard that the show manager of the Pyramid needed a trained camel, she got in touch with me. That's how I got this gig.

"Baby Bloom and Sally were the best of friends when they arrived at the ranch. Of course, Sally stayed on. Baby Bloom left about a year after you were born. She left me her guitar as payment for room and board. I told her she didn't have to do such a thing, but she said that she had to do something nice for the man who took such good care of Sally. That's her guitar I still play.

"She told me that leaving her guitar at the ranch was the real cause of her success. She said that having that guitar on her lap all the time was like trying to sing and operate a computer at the same time. She said she just had to concentrate on her fingering so hard, she couldn't break out into song. So once she left the guitar at the ranch, she just dropped her hands to her sides and lifted her chin and sounds came out that were shaped like her and not like anyone else. And then since she didn't have to spend her time practicing playing, she started writing music instead."

"I wish I had known that you and Mother are good friends of Trina Rose," I said. "I could have made everyone at Fortnum green with envy. Absolutely green. Chartreuse."

"What would you want to do that for, Bo?"

"To show them."

"To show them what?"

"That I'm not a UW."

I explained to Father that UW meant United Way, and that it meant the scholarship students at Fortnum.

"But you won't be a UW. You'll be F. Hugo Malatesta's stepson."

"No, I won't be. He's not adopting me."

"In any case, he's paying. You won't be a UW."

"Aren't you ashamed to have another man pay for your son's education?" I asked.

Father said, "No."

Trina Rose arrived for rehearsal promptly at two. That was exactly the time she was supposed to. Father said that she was a real pro, and professionals were always on time.

Trina Rose was fat. She was not heavy the way that Mama Rosita was. Trina Rose was fat like a huge scoop of vanilla ice cream that's been at room temperature for a couple of hours. She wore dresses that looked like a parachute with a hole cut in the center for her head and neck. She billowed when she walked.

Father sat quietly in a corner waiting for the crowd that had arrived with Trina Rose to thin out. When it did, she noticed Father and ran toward him with both arms outstretched like a kite fluttering to the ground.

"Woodrow Stubbs, you bloody old fart," she

said. "If I hadn't just had my second breakfast, I would eat you right up. How's that short-haired, long-legged beast of yours? I'm referring to Ahmed, of course. Nothing private intended."

Father laughed and hugged Trina Rose back. "Ahmed's fine," he said. "And so is Sally. Sally just got married."

"Well, I'll be switched," she said. "Sally Ghost married again. I'll bet she caught herself some guy with a billion in the bank and a foot in the grave."

"His name is F. Hugo Malatesta, the First," I said. "And he is rich, but there can be young grandfathers, you know."

Trina Rose looked at me, put a hand on my shoulder and said, "It's Bo!" She turned to Father and said, 'Tell me! It's bloody Bo, isn't it?" Father nodded. Trina Rose came over to me and hugged me so that I was lost in a tangle of arms and sleeves. She didn't let me go. She clutched me to her and rocked me back and forth. Then she pushed me to arm's length still holding me. She studied my face, and then she pulled me to her again. "He's right handsome, Woody," she said. "And he looks bloody normal, too. God, that Sally Ghost doesn't know how lucky she is." I was still crushed against Trina Rose's bosom, and she started rocking me again. Then she pushed me just far enough from her to stretch her arms full length and clamp her hands behind my neck. "Listen, Bo," she said, "did you know that I'm your bloody damn godmother?" I shook my head as best I could. "Well, I bloody well am," she said, "I led your daddy blindfolded out of that bloody hospital. Now I want you to watch my whole damn rehearsal from the minute I arrive on top of bloody Ahmed until I sing my final-most song. And I want you to bloody well know that I'm singing to you, love. This whole rehearsal is for you." Then she said to Father, "Can I have him stay with me, Woody? I have half a hallway full of rooms. I could sleep two in the bathtub alone. You should see it. It's pink marble. Looks like a goddam war memorial. Christ, you can stay too, Woody, if you like. I won't bother with your bloody animal, though." Father did not answer. He had no chance to because she called, "Mordred! Mordred!" Mordred was her bloody manager, I found out. "These two old friends of mine will be moving into my suite. Tell the hotel bloody management."

Father declined. He insisted to Trina Rose that it would be inconvenient for him to be in a high rise so far away from Ahmed.

"You're bloody well tied down to that beast," Trina Rose said. "Well, aren't we all? Tied to one damn beast or another?"

Father then told Trina Rose that just because he couldn't stay in her hotel suite was no reason for me not to.

So I did.

I moved into Suite 1424 where there were two

bedrooms as well as the sofa in the living room making into a bed. I slept in a bed that was room-sized in a room that was pool-sized, Olympic pool-sized.

Once there I settled into my Vegas routine. I called it my Vegas routine, not Las Vegas, because all the pros drop the *Las*. It was not what you would call a basic routine because the hours were not basic and because Trina Rose is no routine person. Except when she was on stage. And then she made sure that everything moved like clockwork. And she had to OK everything down to the stage lights. As a matter of fact, to hear her carry on about them, you would think that she was Picasso and the stage lights were tubes of paint. "They set the whole bloody mood," she explained. And then she whispered in my ear, "and if they ain't right, I can look downright obese right up there on stage." I asked no further questions. How should I know how she sees herself?

My Trina Rose Vegas Routine:

I got up about ten in the morning. Trina Rose would still be asleep. I would order room service. I would get dressed and wait for room service out in the hall, because I didn't want them to knock and possibly wake up Trina Rose. They would bring whatever I ordered. I signed my name and Room 1424 and added TIP $2.00, because Trina Rose told me to do that. I would carry my tray into the living room and eat it all up.

Trina Rose worked very hard and very long and she deserved her sleep. She did everything long and hard, including sleep.

After breakfast I would go down to the hotel lobby and watch the people. People from all over the world come to Vegas, but people from the United States come the most. The lobby of the Pyramid Hotel had an easel near the registration desk, and on the easel was a sign that told what meetings were being held in what convention rooms. From where I sat in the lobby, I could see the registration desk as well as the gambling casino. Since I was under-aged, I was not allowed to enter the casino, but I could watch. The cashiers give the people who are playing the slot machines their coins in a paper cup. The people who play roulette or blackjack get chips. There is something unreal about everything in Vegas, but nothing seems more unreal than the money.

There were three kinds of people who regis-tered: one, the people who were worried about the cost of everything; they spent their time checking on the price of their rooms. They would later wander down to the gambling casino and take the free cigarettes whether they smoked or not. Two, the people who wanted to seriously gamble; they pulled on a few slot machines before they even lo-cated their luggage or checked into their rooms. And third, the conventioneers. They stayed at the registration counter the longest because (1) they all seemed to arrive at the same time, (2) they had as many as four people (sometimes from four different states) staying in one room, (3) they arrived so early that the rooms had not been cleaned up from the people before them.

I got my Vegas education from noon until about one-thirty when I would return to Suite 1424 to start the awakening process, for Trina Rose would start getting up about two o'clock in the afternoon, and I liked to be back in the suite when it started.

First there came a ring on the telephone from Mordred, her manager. I would answer the phone and assure Mordred a basic fifteen times that I would indeed see to it that Trina Rose would get up that very day. I would then go into her bedroom and call her name and gently poke her until she began to move. She moved wondrously slow. First she set all the bedsheets to rippling. A lot of things about Trina Rose rippled. Her laughter, her stomach, and most especially her singing. When the rhythms of her getting-up movements broadened from ripples to waves, I called room service and ordered a large glass of orange juice and a pot of coffee to be delivered. Slowly, slowly, one eye, one shoulder, one arm showed itself above the covers, and finally Trina Rose rose. It was like she gave birth to a new self every day. By the time she was sitting up in bed, room service had delivered the juice and the coffee, and I had signed my name and Room 1424 and had added TIP $2.00.

Then I carried the tray into her room and poured a waterglass full of juice. Trina Rose would drink it, and I would pour her a cup of coffee. She would take the coffee and issue her first *bloody* of the day. Something like this: "There was a bloody capacity crowd last night," she would say. "I sang my bloody lungs out—not because I loved them. I had to, just to be heard."

Then we would talk. I was anxious to learn about when she was Baby Bloom and had traveled with my mother from Frisco to Taos, and although she told me some things, she never told me enough to give me a clear picture of how my tailored mother had once been a girl named Sally Ghost. She asked about me, and what I had been doing since I was Maximilian and mother was Sarah, and I found that what I talked about the most were the things that had happened to me since Smilax.

When I told her about Manuelo, she said, "Tough, Bo, tough. The only thing you can bloody do is to remember how much you hate yourself sometimes and be careful not be such a sticky smart ass next time."

When I told her about Sabrina and Lilly, the travel agents and the Lambda Gammas, the freaks and the eccentrics, she said, "Now, that Sabrina sounds like someone I'd like to know. Take me. If

I weren't so bloody talented, I'd just be a fat lady who sings. You've either got to be two kinds of freak or none at all."

When I told her about Denver and Ruthie Britten and how Father had abandoned me, she said, "Abandoned you?"

"What would you call it?"

"Oh, Bo," she said, "Woodrow bloody Stubbs is the last person in the world that you can say abandons anyone."

"You're probably thinking of Ahmed and how he didn't abandon Ahmed after Lucky Blue ran off with Dove and left him at the ranch."

"I'm only partly thinking of that," Trina Rose said. "Only partly."

After we talked and after Trina Rose drank all her coffee and her juice, she would get up to shower and to dress. She mostly just got dressed in a bathrobe. While she was doing that, I would call room service and order her real breakfast and my lunch. We sat at a table in the living room to eat that.

After that Mordred would come and discuss business, or she would actually put on some out-of-door clothes, which—truth to tell—did not look too different from her housecoats, and we would go out to shop.

Trina Rose loved big discount drugstores. She bought lipsticks and junk jewelry and hair brushes for herself. She bought combs and wallets and key chains for me. One drugstore had a record department, and Trina Rose took out a felt tip pen and autographed all her own albums. At the check-out counter, she said, "Some bloody broad just signed her name all over Trina Rose's albums. No harm done. It's just on the cello wrap. It'll pull right off."

The checkout girl said, "There's more weirdos in this town than in a state mental institution."

Trina Rose leaned over the counter to whisper in the girl's ear, "Listen, dear, if you want me to, I'll just go on back there and write *not* on top of every bloody one of those Trina Rose autographs. Everyone in his right mind knows that there's no such person as Trina Rose. I'm the real thing: me, Catarina Rosenblum." She then pushed her VISA card with the name CATARINA ROSENBLUM under the girl's nose.

"Sure, honey," the girl said.

To okay the credit card the girl had to ring for the manager. While she was waiting, she kept glancing over at us. Trina Rose turned to me and said, "Bo, honey, let's you and me buy all those autographed bloody albums. Those signatures could be real. You go on back and pick them out for us."

There were seven of them, and I brought them up to the counter. By then the manager was there, too.

"Add these to my bill," Trina Rose said.

The manager asked for three pieces of identification and okayed the bill. Trina Rose took the ball point pen and signed *Catarina Rosenblum,* and then took a felt tip pen out and signed *Trina Rose* under that.

"They do match," I said.

Whereupon Trina Rose burst into song. *"Cry! Cry! Cry for baby love,"* she sang in that voice of hers, the likes of which there is no basic other.

Then as the cashier and the manager checked the charge slip with *Trina Rose* scrawled across it, we walked out. Just remembering the look on the face of the clerk and her manager was a day's entertainment.

Wherever we might be during the day, you could be sure that Trina Rose was backstage by five-thirty. She was loose and unhurried and always on time. She was something remarkable. Everyone backstage was, but she was the most.

Part of my Vegas routine was my reunion with Father, which took place every evening backstage before the early show. I would help him decorate Ahmed with pompoms in a color that matched Trina Rose's mood or costume. After we sent Ahmed on stage with his star on top, Father and I waited until Ahmed was led backstage by one of the showgirls while Trina Rose stayed on stage and belted out one song after another.

I found the showgirls interesting. After only a few performances, I found them more interesting than what they weren't wearing.

I concluded that there are two kinds of chorus girls: rose ones and gray ones. And their color has nothing to do with their color. It has to do with their behavior. The gray ones are hard.

"You're right," Father said. "You can almost see their steel core."

Trina Rose, the star of the show, was rose and violet with just enough brown and gray to make shadows. Stars are variegated people.

I went up to our suite after the early show and ordered room service. Trina Rose and Father would come along, and we'd have supper in the living room. They'd go back down for the midnight show, but I wouldn't. I was a growing boy, and I had to take care of my health. I would stay in the suite and read or watch TV or think.

There was a lot to think about. There was my mother most of all. Having her marry F. Hugo Malatesta had seemed the most normal thing in the world while I was in Havemyer. And that seeming normal made her being friends with Trina Rose and her once being Sally Ghost seem abnormal. I wouldn't say freakish. Maybe I would say freakish.

One evening after dinner when Father and Trina Rose had returned backstage, I remembered that I had left a paperback book from that day's shopping trip in our hotel suite. I wanted it to read while we waited backstage, so I went upstairs to get it. When I returned, I heard Trina Rose saying, "I would have thought that Sally Ghost would bloody well have told him by now."

Father said, "I don't mind. She's not ready to."

"Why do you say that?"

"It seems she told him that her parents died in an auto accident."

"Was that after your divorce she told him that?" There was a pause. Father must have nodded. Then Trina Rose said, "She'll make it into respectability land with this F. Hugo Fart. I just don't know, Woody. I just don't bloody know. Sally Ghost was my good friend, but I don't know Sarah Jane Whitley Stubbs Malatesta at all. But what the hell. I like the kid. Balls! Woody. I goddam love that kid."

They stopped talking as soon as they saw me. I said nothing because I knew that I would upset Trina Rose, and she didn't take kindly to being upset before a performance. I just said, "hi!" as though I hadn't heard anything, and I hung around and waited for her and Ahmed to go onstage before I asked my Father.

"Do you mean that Mother lied when she told me her parents died in an auto crash?"

Father shrugged. "I don't know," he said. "Maybe your mother lied, but maybe they died."

"Wouldn't you think you would care enough to find out and at least send a sympathy card? After all, Mother was your wife; Mother is the mother of your child. That's me, in case no one told you."

"I have never met your mother's parents. I didn't even know their name until your mother and I applied for a marriage license. The girl who came to stay at the ranch in Taos was known to me as Sally Ghost, and I didn't ask questions."

"I notice that you don't."

"Don't what?"

"Ask questions."

"When we went to get the marriage license, I found out that your mother's real name was Sarah Jane Whitley."

"Don't you think that Grandma and Grandpa Whitley would have wanted to send congratulations? Or a wedding present?"

"I don't think so."

"Why not?"

"Your mother tried calling them, and they wouldn't talk to her."

"Why wouldn't they?"

"Do you know what pregnant is?" he asked.

I was shocked. I said, "That shows how little you know about me. Of course I know what *pregnant* is."

"Of course you do. I shouldn't have asked. You see, when I do ask questions, I ask the wrong ones. But the thing of it is this: your mother was pregnant when we got married."

I was a little bit shocked at that. Of course, they never mentioned their wedding date because they never celebrated it. Of course, if they had not gotten divorced and had celebrated their wedding date, I could have counted the months between my birth and their wedding and found out that I was pre-expected. I swallowed my surprise and said to Father. "So what? I've joined the crowd. I'll bet half the first-borns at Fortnum School can't add nine months between the time their parents got married and the time they were born. Is that what made Mother's parents ashamed? Do you think she lied about her parents dying in an auto crash?"

"I don't know, Bo. Maybe they rejected her again, and she had to pretend to herself they were dead. I haven't any idea at all about them. No idea if they're alive or dead."

The chorus girl who led Ahmed on stage returned with him. Father took the guide rope from her and thanked her. Then he began loosening Ahmed's bridle, and I went up to Room 1424 to think.

6

Instead of ordering room service the next morning, I put on my Fortnum blazer and went to the coffee shop, which was called the Gizeh Coffee Shoppe. On my way to the Gizeh I passed the bulletin board with the list of the day's activities. I read it out of habit. At the top it said:

WELCOME
Southern Association, Real Estate Dealers
Registration: 9:00–2:00 Luxor Room
Banquet: 7 p.m. The Nile Ballroom

FAREWELL LUNCHEON:
U.S. CONFERENCE OF PHYSICAL THERAPISTS
12:30 p.m. Cleopatra Hall
SEE TRINA ROSE IN ARABIAN CHIC
TWO SHOWS NIGHTLY
7:00 p.m. and Midnight
Make your reservation at Courtesy
Desk in Karnak Lobby

While I waited for my order to arrive, I saw Sabrina enter the Gizeh Coffee Shoppe and stand by the register where a sign said, "Please wait for hostess to seat you." I saw the hostess return from seating two other people, and as she passed my table, I called to her and asked her please to show Sabrina to my table.

"Your sister?" the hostess asked.

I nodded.

The hostess nodded to Sabrina and said, "This way, please." She brought her to my table. I didn't turn around, but she recognized me.

"Maximilian," she said. "What a surprise."

"Yes," I said. "I was born a surprise."

She sat down across from me. "Mother will be along in a minute," she said.

"Don't tell me," I said. "Let me guess. You're here for the Conference of the Southern Association of Real Estate Dealers, and let me also guess there's been some confusion with your conference registration." She started to say something, but I held my hand up to her. "And let me guess further than that. For some reason the conference has forgotten to give you and your mother—whatever your names are this time—your proper identification tags. But your mother will get duplicates. Handwritten. She's at the registration desk straightening things out now. Is that right?" I asked. "A basic *yes* answer will do."

"No," she said, "we're here for the U.S. Conference of Physical Therapists."

"Oh!" I said. "Then you will be having your

farewell luncheon at twelve-thirty p.m. And let me guess again. Your bags will be packed. That's what your mother is doing right now. And in all the confusion of everyone leaving the convention after the farewell luncheon, you two will also leave. But you two will leave without paying your bill."

"Yes," she said simply, "we do that. There's always a lot of confusion at check-out time. We count on that. Mother was near panic in Dallas when I visited you. I'll bet it takes days for the hotel to discover that we've skipped out."

"Don't you know? Don't they write you dunning letters?"

"When the hotel finds that we've slipped out, they have to contact the sponsoring organization. We charge everything to them."

"Doesn't the organization dun you?"

"Dun who? Lilly Pacsek or Lilly Miller or Lilly . . ."

"You've made your point."

"Don't the hotels ask for identification?"

"Not when you're a star. Lilly always books herself in as a featured speaker or a workshop leader. Sometimes she has flowers sent to our room with the best wishes of the organization."

"Don't the hotels recognize you?"

"Not a chance. There are enough conventions in enough hotels to go for years without repeats. Besides, hotels change management almost as often as they change bed linen. Mother and I are concentrating on the West this year. We wanted to explore this part of the United States. The year before last we did the Northeast. New York is very expensive. Imagine how expensive it would have been if we had paid for everything."

The waitress brought my order and pulled out her pad to take Sabrina's. "I'll be ordering for my mother, too," Sabrina said.

"I'll be back," the waitress said.

"Never mind," I said, pulling out my room key. "Put the whole thing on my check."

The waitress looked at my key number. "Hmmm," she said. "The penthouse."

"Yes," I said, slipping it into my blazer pocket.

"A penthouse," Sabrina said. "What happened? Did Ahmed demand rights to a Jacuzi or something? I understand Jacuzis are very big in Las Vegas."

"Everything is very big in Vegas," I said. "Tits, tips. Everything is big. Nothing seems real."

I then told her what we were doing in Vegas, how undeluxe, unglamorous, unhousebroken Ahmed had made it into show business. And then I told her about how Trina Rose was my godmother, which was why I was staying in the penthouse. I was ready to tell her the news I had learned last night when Lilly appeared in the doorway of the Gizeh Room. Sabrina, who was facing that direction, waved her mother over to our table.

Lilly was dressed in a tailored navy blue skirt

and a white blouse. She had tied a scarf around her neck so that it looked like something halfway between a necktie and a ruffle. And her hair was pulled straight back into a bun. She had a jacket thrown over her shoulder. Her HELLO badge was pinned on the jacket. She slipped it off, but not before I read LILLY MILLER, Leafneck, Wisconsin.

After saying how good it was and what a surprise it was to see me, Lilly said to Sabrina, "I have the best possible news, dear. I was talking to a colleague, and she said that the twins are doing fine. They still don't have skulls; they still wear padded bonnets, but they say *Mama* and *Dada* and they play with each other. They still can't sit up or walk, but she's working on that. Isn't that just grand?"

"Your colleague was a physical therapist?" I asked.

"Yes. She's one who's working with the twins. They were Siamese, joined at the top of their skulls, you know."

I said that I didn't know.

Sabrina said, "I'm glad you got the report, Mother. If they keep up the good work, I may have to take them out of my freak file," she said.

Lilly asked how Woody and Ahmed were, and I told her that Ahmed was now in show business.

"Trina Rose is Maximilian's godmother," Sabrina said. "He's staying in her suite."

"Imagine him not saying anything about that," Lilly said.

"I didn't know," I said.

After our breakfasts had been ordered, delivered and eaten, I took the check. I wrote Room 1424 and TIP $5.00 and signed my name. Lilly and Sabrina thanked me, and then Lilly excused herself saying that she had to attend to some packing. I gave Sabrina a knowing nod. Sabrina and I left the restaurant. "Thanks for breakfast," she said. "We don't usually have to pay for any of our meals after Mother makes contacts. If we don't find someone to treat us, we eat in the hotel and charge it to our room, but Lilly usually lines up someone to treat us to lunch, to cocktails, to everything except the banquets and luncheons, where there are speakers and where the cost is prepaid in our convention fee—which we don't pay anyway."

I asked Sabrina if she would please come sit by the hotel pool with me. "I look down on it from our room, and it's always empty. We can be alone there, except for the towel boys and the cocktail waitresses. I want to talk to you," I said.

She said she would come and agreed to meet at the elevator on the pool level.

I ran up to Suite 1424 and put on the bathing suit Trina Rose had bought me on one of our discount drugstore shopping sprees. Then I raced back out and waited by the pool elevator. Sabrina did not come. I used a house phone and called the registration desk to find out her room number, remembering that they were registered under the name of Miller this time. Lilly answered the phone. She told me that yes, Sabrina was there, but she was not feeling well, that she, Lilly, was just on her way down to tell me that Sabrina could not be meeting me.

"Mrs. Miller, Mrs. Anderson, Mrs. Pacsek. Lilly," I said. "Sabrina did not tell me what was going on. I guessed. I have a very logical mind. Please let her come to the pool. I promise you I won't blow your cover. I promise you Sabrina will be waiting by the door of Cleopatra Hall by the time your farewell luncheon begins."

"But what about Trina Rose? You know the star of the show. She's in the employ of the hotel. You're even related to her."

"Mrs. Miller, Mrs. Ander—"

"Lilly."

"Lilly. I can assure you that Trina Rose has more secrets than the chairman of the CIA. And some of them are just as important. She wouldn't want to know yours."

"But I wouldn't want a nice gentleman like your father to think that I'm doing something . . ."

"I promise you I will not tell my father," I said.

I asked Sabrina how long she and her mother had been living like this.

"Three summers," she answered. "What do you think Mother does in the winter?"

I thought about jobs that had long vacations. I could only think of schoolteacher, so that is what I guessed.

"No. We go out only three weeks in the summer. We'll drive home from here."

"I can't guess what your mother is. It's hard to tell. She seems to be everything she pretends to be."

"She is. My mother is an eight hundred number."

"You mean that your mother is toll free?"

"That's the least of what I mean," she said. "Suppose you get a catalogue from Bloomingdale's Department Store in New York and another one from Neiman Marcus in Dallas and another from a gift shop in New Hampshire. All of them will invite you to 'Telephone your order toll-free twenty-four hours a day, seven days a week. Use our toll-free number. Call 1-800 . . . anywhere in the Continental United States.' Someone has to be there to answer the phone, and for eight hours a day Lilly is a someone. She sits in a room with ninety-nine other people. Each of them has about eighty catalogues that they take orders from. It is the most anonymous job in the world, speaking to people you'll never know and who will never know you. Always available. Always a polite voice. Never a face. Never a personality. Never a before. Never an after."

"Airlines and hotel chains also have eight hundred numbers."

"Yes. They are one degree less anonymous because they handle only one product, but they still sit in a room with a hundred people and they are just a polite voice that you talk to once, that you don't know where it's coming from."

"Where do you come from?"

"Omaha. That's the home of the catalogue eight hundred numbers."

"How did you get started doing conventions?"

"There was a convention in Omaha. It was a convention of meat packers. Their convention headquarters was at the Howard Johnson Motel. That night was Mother's birthday, and we had decided to go out to celebrate. It was raining, and we ran inside the first door we came to after we parked the car. And there we were in the hall leading to the ballroom. Everyone was milling around having drinks, and some old gentleman came up to Mother and introduced himself and kept looking at Mother's bosom. Later we realized that he was looking for her HELLO badge, and when he went to introduce her to someone else, Mother said she left it in her room. The gentlemen knocked themselves out bringing Mother drinks and bringing me Coca-Colas. When the banquet was ready to start, we waited until almost everyone was seated, and we saw there were empty places. We knew they had already been paid for, so we sat down and were served just like everyone else. Mother and I enjoyed the whole evening.

"When Mother got home from work the next day, we got dressed up again and headed for the Howard Johnson's. We never even discussed it with each other. Everyone welcomed us back, and we enjoyed the wine and cheese. There was always Coke for me.

"That summer we decided to go convention-eering. We decide what time we want to take our vacation, and what towns we want to visit. Then Mother calls the eight hundred numbers of several large motel chains in those cities and asks if their convention rooms are available for those dates. If they say they are not, she pretends to be upset and politely asks what organization is meeting there. When we find out, we begin our research.

"We go to the library. There is a book in the library called *The Encyclopedia of Associations*. It gives the addresses and the names of 13,589 organizations, all you could ever think of. And some you never could."

"Name one I never could."

"How about The American Council of Spotted Asses in Fishtail, Montana? Or how about The National Button Society of Akron, Ohio? It has both a junior section and a shut-in section."

"Have you ever been to a convention of spotted asses?"

"Of course not. It's got only ninety members. Lilly and I, as well as the asses, would be spotted. No, we choose large and preferably rich organizations. Mother prefers professional ones; I, business ones. The professional ones are more interesting, but the business ones are freer with the money.

"Mother finds out what groups are meeting in the towns we want to visit, and she writes some letters of inquiry so that we can get letters back. We reproduce their letterheads and send the hotel a letter on the faked stationery, saying that Lilly will be arriving at such and such a time and that she is to be a speaker or a workshop leader, and that the hotel is to charge her bill to the organization. Then she signs the president's name with a slash and some initials, which tells the people that some secretary signed the correspondence in the boss's absence. You get the president's name from the same encyclopedia."

"We appear at the convention and check into our room. We carry a supply of various HELLO badges, but sometimes—like at the travel agents convention—you need a special one to get on and off the convention floor. That's when Lilly goes into her act about the lost badges and so on. Sometimes, she picks a last name from the list at the registration desk. Lilly can read just about anything upside down. Sometimes she has to produce a copy of the letter she wrote. One thing or another always works.

"After that it's easy. We simply appear at the meetings and at the banquets.

"Lilly loves the research. She loves being a travel agent or a physical therapist. She loves being something other than anonymous, other than an eight hundred number. I think conventions are part of the war against anonymity. I'll bet small countries don't have them."

"Have you ever been caught?"

"You're the first."

"Don't you just hate never being yourself?"

"I am *always* myself. I know when I'm pretending. Pretending is perfectly normal for me." She looked at me with those eyes that looked like you could float an ocean liner in and then said, "It's you, Maximilian Stubbs, who doesn't know who you are."

"I don't know what makes you say that."

"Your HELLO badge."

"What do you mean? I don't have a HELLO badge."

"Yes you do. It's always the same. It's always the Fortnum crest on your blue blazer. It's like you have to look at that to know who you are."

"I do not."

"Yes, you do."

"I never pretend to be something I'm not. It even got me into trouble with a kid named Manuelo when we were in Tulsa."

"Everyone pretends. Everyone with everyone some of the time and everyone with some people all of the time. Except freaks. They're the only ones who can't pretend. But I've told you that."

"I don't think Trina Rose pretends."

"What do you call performing?"

"But that's part of her. If it's pretend, it's real."

Sabrina smiled. "Yes, it is."

"Woody doesn't pretend."

"Yes, he does, Max. Woody is too real not to have some pretend about him."

"What's your real name?" I asked.

"Maybe it's Pacsek," she said. "And maybe it's Stubbs."

"You are infuriating," I said.

It was 12:15. Sabrina got up and said, "Just call any eight hundred number. One of them is bound to be my mother."

Then Sabrina left.

When I went back to Suite 1424, Trina Rose was still asleep. The first call from Mordred still had not come. I shook her gently and began the awakening process. It was a little early, but I wanted to talk to her.

After Trina Rose had had her second cup of coffee, I said, "I just saw Sabrina. She and her mother were at a convention of physical therapists."

"Invite them up," Trina Rose said. "I'd like to meet them."

"They'll be leaving in a few minutes," I said. "I had a talk with Sabrina. I also had a talk with Father, and I want to know about when my mother was Sally Ghost."

"That's when I met her. She was this lost girl,

freaked out and scared. I had an old station wagon, and we teamed up and headed from San Francisco to New Mexico. Everyone said that there was good clean air outside Taos, and that's where I took Sally Ghost.

"Woody took us in and gave us everything we needed: food and love and kindness. He gave that to everyone who crashed his place, but Sally Ghost was special to him from the minute we arrived. Everyone saw it. She became his pet."

"Like Ahmed?"

"No. Much more than bloody Ahmed."

"I know about them," I said.

"Know what, Love?"

"Know that my mother was pregnant when they got married."

"Do you know that now, Love?"

"Yes. I just found out. Last night."

"That's the kind of guy bloody ole Woody is. He married Sally Ghost and made her Mrs. Woodrow Stubbs. He was crazy about that girl, and he loved you like you was his very own. Just the way he did Sally Ghost."

"What do you mean? He loved me like I was his very own? My mother was pregnant when they got married."

"Yes. But not by him, Love. Not by him. Sally Ghost was pregnant when we arrived at the ranch. Didn't he tell you that, Love?"

There was an air space in my throat that

swelled like a small balloon, and my heart developed sharp edges and began flipping like a match box bruising me inside. I swallowed that balloon and let it tamp down all the screaming that was inside of me. I did not cry.

"Didn't you know that, Love?" Trina Rose asked.

"No," I said, fighting that balloon that had risen again in my throat. "Then tell me, Trina Rose, who is my father?"

"Why, I'd say Woody is. Wouldn't you, Love?"

I asked nothing more.

There were three more days before I was to fly back to Havemyer. I thought I might check out of Suite 1424 and move into the camper so that I could spend more time with Woody. But I decided against that. I decided instead to play it the same way as I had been, to keep up my Trina Rose Vegas routine, and that is what I did. There was no reason to worry Woody by letting him know what I knew. There were many questions to be asked, but I would ask them slowly, and I would start asking them in Pennsylvania. I would just enjoy being his son, Bo, even if I didn't enjoy his camel.

On our last shopping trip, Trina Rose decided to buy Mother and Mr. Malatesta a wedding present. True to Trina Rose's style, she bought them something huge that they wouldn't use. She bought them an electric wok and told me to take it back on the plane with me. It sat between Woody and me as we drove to the airport.

Woody was wearing his Pinocchio hat and the red scarf around his neck. I wore one of my cowboy shirts and my new boots and I had my blazer thrown over my lap. Woody pulled a clipping from his shirt pocket. "I found this in the paper today," he said, handing it over to me.

The article was about the tallest man in the world, eight feet two inches. He had just died. He was known as the gentle giant.

I reached across the wok box and took it from him.

"Thought you might like to save it for Sabrina."

"Thanks," I said. I laid it on the wok box that was between us and folded it. When I picked it back up I saw printed on the wok carton: ORDER REPLACEMENT OR ADDITIONAL PARTS. CALL 1-800-298-4520, 24 HOURS A DAY, INCLUDING SUNDAYS.

"I don't know if Sabrina collects dead freaks," I said. "Besides, I don't know how to get in touch with her."

"It wouldn't surprise me if she gets in touch with you," he said. "She knows who you are."

"Yeah," I said. "I think she thinks she does."

I tucked the clipping into the breast pocket of my Fortnum blazer and put my blazer on top of the wok box. I lifted both of them up and shifted them to my other side. Then I slid over, closer to Woody. He lifted an arm from the steering wheel and pulled me to him, and I rested against him as we drove to the airport.